The Painter's Wife

Monique Durand

Translated by Sheila Fischman

Talonbooks • Vancouver

Talonbooks
P.O. Box 2076, Vancouver, British Columbia, Canada V6B 3S3
www.talonbooks.com

Typeset in Scala and printed and bound in Canada.

First Printing: 2006

The publisher gratefully acknowledges the financial support of the Canada Council for the Arts; the Government of Canada through the Book Publishing Industry Development Program; and the Province of British Columbia through the British Columbia Arts Council for our publishing activities.

La femme du peintre by Monique Durand was first published in French by Le Serpent à Plumes, Paris, France. Financial support for this translation provided by the Canada Council for the Arts and the Department of Canadian Heritage through the Book Publishing Industry Development Program.

Library and Archives Canada Cataloguing in Publication

Durand, Monique, 1953–
[Femme du peintre. English]
The painter's wife / Monique Durand ; translated by Sheila Fischman.

Translation of: La femme du peintre.
ISBN 0-88922-535-4

I. Fischman, Sheila II. Title.

PS8557.U73234F4413 2006 C843'.54 C2005-906202-9

ISBN-10: 0-88922-535-4
ISBN-13: 978-0-88922-535-0

Contents

for Madeleine Gagnon

for Catherine, 17, François, 15,
Jean-Philippe, 7, Marie-Ève, 5,
Charlotte, 14

In memory of Evelyn Rowat Marcil,
some of whose experiences,
in the course of a remarkable life,
inspired this work of fiction.

Prologue

NOVEMBER, 1993. Toronto Crematorium. Evelyn, her friend Nicolas at her side, stands over the body of René, which is covered with a white sheet. She touches the body: “He’s cold.” Nicolas, moved, sets down on the remains a bouquet of flowers from which he’s forgotten to remove the transparent cellophane wrapping. “No, no, no!” says Evelyn, nearly shouting. “You have to take off the paper!” Nicolas, nervous and awkward, complies, the cellophane resists, the remains are already on their way to fire and ash.

How can I be thinking at a moment like this about the evening when I took you to the Paradis for dinner, because their french-fried potatoes were so good, or about turning into the wrong lane at an intersection when your face, Evelyn, changed in a second from an angel’s to a demon’s? I was sent reeling for long moments, stunned by your callousness, discovering the tyrant in you as you shifted impatiently in your seat. “No, no, no, not there!” After that incident, the Paradis’s famous potatoes seemed to me no more than miserable greasy cinders, the remains of some buried torment.

Nicolas’s hands are shaking. The paper resists. Evelyn is furious. His clumsiness grows with her exasperation.

In the madness of the moment, Evelyn, it’s startling, I hear music. Applause. From the crowd attending Vladimir Horowitz’s historic Moscow recital. The pianist’s return to his native Russia and at the same time, his farewell. The date is 20 April 1986. He has just finished the “Reverie,” from Schumann’s *Scenes from Childhood*. The audience is on its feet. Weeping. Moaning. Even the Soviet officials, in close order in the orchestra and the balconies, a forest of braid and suits at attention, even those sinister puppets can't resist the old man's sublime performance. Their tears gleam in the lights, then fall like an early scattering of autumn snow. The gloom of the nomenklatura and the collective farms has just touched the corona of the sun.

Outside, huddling under umbrellas, hundreds gathered in front of the Conservatory. Not one note of music reaches them, but they hear everything. Two hundred students have managed to cross the security cordons and have stormed the aisles of the concert hall. During the first Scarlatti sonata, the police will try to dislodge them. In vain.

Horowitz himself, in his late eighties now, so many years an exile, sends kisses with the old hands of a genius. Old hands so flexible they can bend backwards, like rolling eyes, finger bones that are extendable, retractable, bent. Briefly, Horowitz, lifted from the earth by the audience's cries, clutches at his piano to keep from taking flight.

The audience is speechless, transfixed, spellbound, reduced to an exclamation. Electric shock. State of grace. Horowitz bows to the delirious crowd, choked with emotion. He seems to be saying that he won't come back, that he is too old, too weary, because of absence and false hopes. The spectators protest.

What they are expressing, Evelyn, is desire, pure and simple. How else describe this trance of love and farewells? From the house appear roses, hundreds of roses. They are desire flying up to the roof of heaven, desire of men and women together. Indeed, there are no longer men and women in this hall, only the human condition of tangled flesh and hopes.

How can they go on living afterwards, Evelyn, do you know? How can they come back down to our drab and feverless earth? And he, the genius with the backward bending hands, what will he do?

In the midst of the applause and the tears, the body of René Marcil disappears, carried off by the funerary equipment.

Following the body, a torn bouquet of flowers, its cellophane wrapping hanging down below the dead man's head.

Part One

Harsh Freedom

The Apprentice Years

1

Is it possible to transmit one generation's inflexibility to the next, through the obscure work of repetition, against one's wishes and against one's will? And is it possible that Evelyn's harshness was in reality her mother's, and before that her grandmother's, left to lie fallow until the wind of atavism has scattered the seeds in age?

The year is 1935. It is in the austere kitchen of a house in Sandwich, a colourless excrescence of the city of Windsor, Ontario, that Evelyn will endure the final thrashing of her life. Because of a word, a simple word: *respect*. Thinking she is engaged in an uncommon exchange with Naomi, the young girl suggests that the term represents more than the simple notion of courtesy. Naomi enters then into a tidal wave of wrath. Her milky skin turns crimson. Her cheeks become two enormous wine stains beneath eyes creased in anger. She grabs the wide leather belt that is always more or less within reach and lashes Evelyn's calves until they bleed. That day, the blows hiss—mark of great combats—all the way to her thighs.

One blow. Two of diamonds. Three blows. Four of clubs. Five blows. Six. Jack of spades. "Lift your skirt! Hurry up!" Queen of hearts. "This will teach you ... " Joker.

Then, peering suddenly at her watch, Naomi quickly slips away. In time for her bridge game with Elizabeth and the Delaney sisters.

That time was the last. Starting then, Evelyn developed a kind of contemptuous indifference towards her mother that would take years to refine, a youthful work that was constantly restarted, reworked, polished in the dark glare of her resolve. A cleverly measured concoction of brutal detachment and concern with protecting herself. An essential oil, secreted dispassionately by her being, that in due course—or so she thought—would save her.

While others, faced with the unbearable, choose denial and lightness, she, Evelyn Rowat, would be tough.

2

THE YEAR IS 1936. Paul's career brings the Rowat family to the Town of Mount Royal, posh appendix of Montreal, an affluent town inhabited by Anglo-Saxons. This is the fourth move in Evelyn's young life, with all the deracination from which a young heart, thirsty for stability, can suffer.

Unlike Naomi, who can easily and nearly instantaneously forge new ties, reinventing her social life as the spider spins her web from place to place, a new network of crowbars, pliers, vises. While the faces around Naomi change, the settings and decoration of tennis clubs and Baptist church basements do barely, and not at all the colour of the playing cards. Toronto, Montreal, Sandwich, the Town of Mount Royal—all the same pointless battle: ace of spades against jack of diamonds.

Naomi serves tea every evening to guests as impenetrable as herself. One tea, two winning tricks, three hands, then they leave. After that, she goes up to her room, which is as immaculately pale as the tight collar that rises from the base of her neck.

Every night, invariably, Evelyn hears the measured footsteps of her mother fluttering in her skirts that are as cold as the nights she spends with her husband. Cold and dry. Nights and days of convenience, in the image of their marriage.

Younger, Evelyn waited. How many days, how many nights, how many years did she wait for the smallest sign of affection? To call to mind the blazing cheek, the quivering bosom of another person against her: her mother. To walk through life with that certainty. A lake, a morning, a mirror. She was waiting, little Evelyn, smoothing her long blonde hair as she waited for a blonde kiss from Naomi. That never came.

Night after night the footsteps continued along their way to the conjugal bedroom. At the same muted rhythm with which the cards were dealt. Till tomorrow, Naomi, my love, my hate.

3

AUTUMN IN THE YEAR 1937. Parade day in the streets of the Town of Mount Royal, ghetto of greenery, of tidiness and calm.

Squeezed into her black dress with the wide pleats and her determination to leave her rank, Naomi, this former rural schoolmistress in Bedford, in Quebec's Eastern Townships, heads the platoon of ladies on parade.

Her body is as stiff and straight as the banner she holds at a forty-five-degree angle in front of her: the colours of the Imperial Order Daughters of the Empire. The women, all similarly bedecked, lead the way, followed by the TMR brass band which presently strikes up "Scotland the Brave." The parade goes past McKenna's Florist Shop, then turns onto Rockland Boulevard.

Above all, don't get too close to the limits of the city of Montreal, city of French Canadians, of factories and tepid dark beer.

Naomi arches her back to appear regal, irreproachable, and to look down as much as possible on everything in life—in particular, everything on the other side of Jean-Talon Street that speaks French.

For the Rowat home does not wish to hear the language of the "Frenchies," that small people of lunch pails and taverns, who plough the belly of Montreal by streetcar just as, in the past, they ploughed their uncultivated land in Dunham or in Saint-Jean-de-Matha, where epileptic sons grow like potatoes.

No. Naomi is grander, more cultivated, stronger. And although her ancestors on both sides fought on the side of the American revolution against England, her IODE banner will veil from her forever the open face of the vulgar land outside the limits of the Town of Mount Royal. Her starched collar will protect her forever from pettiness and from aborted destinies.

The parade moves on, while the final notes of "Scotland the Brave" ring out.

4

SMALL SILVER-RIMMED EYEGLASSES, looking a little like Marcel Proust, a little like Pierre Curie—thus does Paul Rowat appear in a photo taken in 1919, his final year in biochemistry at McGill University. *Summa cum laude.* He is twenty years old. And it is with this angel with the delicate features, overflowing with humanity as certain individuals sometimes do, that the ogress lives.

Goodness was stamped on Paul's very eyes. Patience, too. When the ogress allowed him to breathe for a moment. He played for hours with the little girls, Evelyn and Helen, inventing a thousand enchantments for them, sitting on the living room floor.

He shone at these gentle games, each time becoming a free man again—freedom that he otherwise experienced only in his laboratory, among vials, test tubes and flasks. Released from the cackling regent at whose feet he had long since laid down his arms and thrown in the sponge, crushed by the strongwoman of circuses and salons.

Of course he was not unaware that Naomi's hand was quick with the leather strap. Evelyn had complained about it over the dinner dishes one night, showing him her red and lacerated leg. Her father's voice had become toneless. The only sign that he'd heard: "Your mother is tired," without conviction. His shoulders had shrunk a notch, as if bowed under by misery and shame. Or to ward off blows.

While to Evelyn, her father was quite simply sluggish, limp.

5

WHEN THE GIRLS HAD MATURED SOMEWHAT, Paul began reciting to them a poem by Yeats, whom he had just discovered, fascinated.

The trees are in their autumn beauty,
The woodland paths are dry.
Under the October twilight the water
Mirrors a still sky;
Upon the brimming water among the stones
Are nine-and-fifty swans.

Always the same poem, "The Wild Swans at Coole." And the same lines, declaimed with a touch of emphasis in his voice where his two adored little girls stretch out languidly. The only softness allowed them in the course of their days, browbeaten by Naomi. The only roundness permitted in the angular world that reigned supreme on Dobie Street in the Town of Mount Royal. Paul emphasized rhythm and rhymes.

I have looked upon those brilliant creatures,
And now my heart is sore.
All's changed since I, hearing at twilight,
The first time on this shore,
The bell-beat of their wings above my head,
Trod with a lighter tread.

And while Madame was dressing to entertain her guests, in anticipation of one of those sumptuous evenings chock-full of "good hands," when she would play a perfect game in the same way that others laid out their opponents on the floor. Paul washed the dinner plates and cutlery. Evelyn and Helen dried them abstractedly, seemingly doing nothing.

But now they drift on the still water,
Mysterious, beautiful;
Among what rushes will they build,
By what lake's edge or pool
Delight men's eyes when I awake some day
To find they have flown away?

He often asked them this riddle: "What's the difference between a Pole, an Italian, an Englishman and an Irishman when they look out the window?" Evelyn would heave an exasperated sigh. This was the moment when Helen would invariably choose to disappear into the living room to play some popular tunes on the piano, before the guests appeared at the door. "All right. The Pole, the Italian and the Englishman see in the grey sky the little patch of blue that will blow away the grey. But when the Irishman looks at a clear blue sky, he sees the little grey cloud that will sweep away the infinity of blue."

And then, just for himself, he would sing softly an old ballad of which he only knew the end of the refrain: "And the stony-hearted sailor was my wife."

6

Eight o'clock on the dot. The bridge players arrive. Naomi comes downstairs from her niche, hair done, dressed to kill, empress of the common herd, a well-trained dog wearing perfume and pince-nez. After stiff greetings, the women embracing like nuns while Paul takes care of their mantillas and muffs, the cards are dealt in a dismal silence troubled only by the tick-tock of the clock. A clock inherited from Naomi's father who, one day at the beginning of the century, left mysteriously for San Francisco and was never seen again. Joseph, vanished into the Pacific coast fog and out of the family phantasmagoria. Naomi was seven at the time.

The time has come for the little girls to go upstairs. Paul reverts to the posture of outgoing and acquiescent patriarch. He who has always blithely hated cards now appraises his hand with a mock-earnest look, "Clubs are trump!" One wish now occupies his cerebellum: that half past ten come quickly and release him so that he too can go up to bed.

And while Naomi peels off her corset in the dark, changing from pomaded poodle into *mater dolorosa* with a long white train—the stripping of skins and fine linen that turns his stomach—Paul prays for her death. But the gods he invokes, who are too much like him, have another good laugh at his spinelessness. His languid deities remain impassive.

Some nights, when the light stays on in the bedroom of one of the children—most often Evelyn's—he would think back to his own bedroom with the dormer windows in the big house in Athelstan. When life still offered food and drink. Then the scent of old freedoms would relax the grip on his throat for a moment. And he'd fall asleep with something like a smile on his face.

7

One afternoon—it was spring and the light was tracing large rectangles of copper and gold on the living room rug—Evelyn caught her mother standing in the middle of the room, Lot's wife crossed through with rays of light and luminescent dust. In a kind of trance, she was listening to Mozart, her forehead offered to the open air, Demeter with rosy flesh. Evelyn was certain it was Mozart because the music she heard made the waters swell in the eyes and in the oceans of the world. For the first time, Evelyn was discovering a face from which all trace of harshness had flown along with the piano's notes. A face on which something clear and damp and opulent had settled, something she could have lapped up. As if a trade wind had passed over the unnatural mother, leaving tender lips pursed in a mottled pout.

Her mother was no longer a nose like Cyrano's, sharp and stiff, but lips, all lips, delicate lips that formed a kind of swell, a wake on either side of her chin. Grace had deigned to stop there for a moment, maybe two, and the dam had given way, loosing torrents of tenderness kept behind the mask, perhaps forever. Through the grace of Mozart, the face that was usually paralysed by haughtiness and smugness had become human again.

No more desert that did not hold before this sudden garden. It was Salieri, steeped in jealousy and misery, melting at the sound of Mozart, Salieri with his stricken face, transfigured by the genius of the man he despised above all others: Mozart, who brought him to his knees, doing with him what he would, like an old rag in the wind. It was the very god of music who finished her off with a final thrust of the sublime.

The face of which Evelyn had a furtive glimpse that afternoon never appeared again.

She bolted before her mother, sensing that she was being observed, could spot her in the doorway opened by the mid-season light.

8

THE YOUNG EVELYN, a little too tall and fleshy, with straight red hair and freckles that are her disgrace, smiles ecstatically in the window of the train that's taking her from the Town of Mount Royal into downtown Montreal. Set free in a flash from her suburban prison into Mile End, "real life," she thinks, just long enough for the train tracks to swallow the perimeter of the mountain—an extinct volcano, apparently—that she often sees re-awakening in her window. Mount Royal expels an enormous torrent of lava right onto TMR. Laughing uncontrollably every time, she imagines her mother transfixed for all eternity at the very moment when she's swooping down on a winning trick around a card table, turned into a small Pompeii of bluff and fantasy.

What Evelyn likes above all are empty trains, because they give her more room to daydream. Incrusted in the last seat in the last car, as if in a hothouse with walls that fit her like a leotard, she sometimes has moments of dizziness, moments of real presence. Blessed with insouciance, her body in tune with her soul, she makes her way, huddled around her joy, joy that comes from she knows not where.

Eyes fixed on the slopes of Mount Royal, she starts to discern the twists and turns of her life that appear in the window of the train. Twists and turns vague in outline, resembling her desire, still unspoken, not to turn out like everyone else.

She is going to see Professor Heimlich, an old Hungarian who gives two drawing classes a week, in the evening. An odd character who will tell her of his childhood, consumed by pogroms and by the Great War, of his years at the École des Beaux-Arts in Paris, then of his arrival in Canada fifteen years ago, through the Port of Halifax.

In control now of her young existence and of her harsh freedom, Evelyn is making her way to the easel and the colours of Professor Heimlich, whose studio is at the corner of Notre-Dame and Guy Streets.

At home, no one ever questions her about her comings and goings. As long as she's home by ten o'clock. Never a "Is everything all right?" Never a "How was it?" At most, two or three rules to observe: the ten o'clock curfew, quiet discipline, respect.

One day, Professor Heimlich will take her to see the four presumably impressionist paintings housed by the Museum of Fine Arts on Sherbrooke Street. And the Rembrandts in the Van Horne collection—the fake Rembrandts. He will show her how to tell true from false. From that teaching, Evelyn will take lessons for life. Disentangle within herself artifice and reality, the pretentious and the genuine. Distinguish the margin from the centre. Root out from the clutter of her pathetic existence that which is important and has yet to come.

9

How do human destinies take shape? Why will Evelyn, quite spontaneously and naturally, seek out the studios of artists and designers? And why will she work so hard at copying clothing ads from the *New York Times*? And go into ecstasy one morning over an ad for lemon pie-filling in the *Saturday Evening Post*, proud that she can recognize it as a genuine oil painting, whereas in her home the only art had been a Turner reproduction in one corner of the living room? What had she imagined for herself in the golden pastry? Or rather, how would that gilding, a morsel of a star fallen onto a newspaper, invent her, Evelyn?

It was actually her sister Helen, four years her junior and a very gifted musician, who should have been eyeing a career as an artist. But she was only interested in making a good match.

Evelyn kept pestering the art director at Eaton's to be given a try-out in his drawing studio. Exasperated, in the summer of 1939, Edgar Smith would finally take her on, in the millinery department.

10

September, 1939. Partly from necessity, partly by chance, Evelyn finds herself in the main lobby of Sir George Williams College, suddenly rooted there while she listens to the young black man rehearsing Chopin's "Revolutionary Étude." She who after being forced to study piano for ten years, at her mother's insistence, has learned to recognize the sublime stands there dumbfounded in the midst of the student traffic, hypnotized by the beauty she is hearing.

While she stands unmoving in Sir George's main lobby, people flow around her like a river's water around a reef. Her eyes are closed. Blocking their way, she's unaware of the students brushing against her, "Sorry!" or going around her, "Excuse me!" or galloping by at her side. She is a dislocated mount and the circus rider is leading her as he pleases. And in the place to which he's taking her there are blue orchids, man-eating flowers, forests of mangroves. The dampness and torpor of tropical swamps.

And while the sound is rising, her whole being becomes aware of an odour; all at once the music has become perfume, just as the sea is sometimes more to be smelled than heard. Fragrance of the beginning of the world, primordial breath that long ago transformed craters into blue water, deserts into gardens, dust into birds, to the point where all of them—plants, fish, animals and humans, too—were set apart, to the point where she too was set apart—Evelyn Rowat who would be born centuries later.

Some part of her life, she knows, is beginning here, now, in the solace that has vanished along with the notes of Chopin.

They married two months later. The pianist, Bernard Leshley, and Evelyn Rowat, the young woman who draws hats for Eaton's store.

They were wed in private, in the presence of the score for the "Revolutionary Étude," Bernard at the piano, Evelyn standing behind him. Not touching, but placing on one another's fingers the chime of silence. Exchanging the brightness, the sharp brightness of an August morning sated with summer. With a blazing keyboard as sole witness. Like a cry of love.

11

EVELYN ARRIVES IN THE HEART OF NEW YORK via the royal road, the one that is most beautiful and stirring. It's early morning, the sun of this beginning of summer in the year 1941, which sets fire to the water of the Upper Bay, split in two by the ferry that goes from Staten Island directly into the belly of the beast. The crossing takes only minutes, during which the astounding forest of tall skyscrapers comes gradually closer. In the distance, Manhattan looks like an enormous, many-layered wedding cake.

The ferry plies its way between Brooklyn on the right and Ellis Island and the Statue of Liberty on the left. Is it the morning that brings down all of Evelyn's defences? Her eyes fill with tears. There it is before her, the mythic Statue of Liberty that she has so often heard about, so often seen in magazines and schoolbooks. She stands there, beckoning Evelyn with her torch, making it move faintly. The young woman responds with a brief nod, as if she were delivering her future to the goddess's arms, entrusting her life to that monumental protection.

In the gold that spatters the morning, the eructations of the beast become clearer, louder. The monster, Manhattan, is there, she can almost touch it, its open mouth showing an enchanting dentition of glass and concrete. Firmly in the saddle of her destiny, in the biting intoxication of youth, Evelyn now belongs to nothing and no one.

Bernard has stayed behind in Montreal to pursue his musical studies. He will come by train to see her once a month.

November, 1941. Two weeks before Pearl Harbor, Evelyn is working as a fashion illustrator at Lord & Taylor. She has just obtained her green card and she earns thirty-five dollars a week—three times her salary at Eaton's in Montreal. Soon she'll have her own studio, with professional models posing for her, an apartment on Fifty-third Street with a piano, the earth, and the whole sky, for her alone. With the authorization of Lord & Taylor's senior management, she can now even sign her drawings, which have started to appear in newspapers and magazines.

12

Montreal, 4 November 1944

Evelyn,

> *I don't know you at all, or very little. I've only seen your fingers run over patterns, explore fabrics, pull up collars, survey cuffs and sleeves, scale the peaks of buttonholes all the way up to the steep summits of hats made of silk and felt. I am coming to New York. Will you accept an invitation from a former Eaton's colleague?*

Is it surprising that these two should fall in love one night, deep inside Central Park? Evelyn Rowat asking only to be gathered up and warmed after a cold childhood and the straitlaced Daughters of the Empire, René Marcil to escape from the closed destiny of taverns, clotheslines and the pious images of his working-class, French-Canadian neighbourhood, Montreal's Saint-Henri. They will melt into love like butter into a rich sauce.

The Museum of Modern Art. They stand rooted in front of the tracery of Van Gogh's sky, mute, fascinated, the sky more than sky of "Starry Night," painted in Provence in 1889. Transhumance of constellations, dancing sardana of brilliant spots above the cypress trees. The earth no longer supports them, they have been swept up by the crystal of Van Gogh's firmament.

Outside is the pre-Christmas madness. Pedestrians parade along Lexington Avenue like hordes of industrious ants in search of a reason to live. A mob.

Inside MOMA though, a man and a woman are dazzled. "Starry Night" opens their eyes, opens the world to them, traces its enigma on their warm flesh.

Outside, thousands and thousands of exhalations emit their wheezing mist that swells the dense condensation formed by the cold above the Hudson River. Tires screech over the hoarfrost and snow. Stores where everything can be bought seethe with impatience.

Inside, though, nothing exists but that which is given. "Starry Night" makes its way into the slightest crack in the hills where thrushes and wild boar doze, at the same time filling the void in the existence of René and Evelyn. Their own futility.

Thirsting for love and cool beer, they go to Rumplemeyer's in Central Park.

They will dine without touching their food, two profiles staring hungrily at each other, already lulled by countless kisses in the icy night of Central Park, where René's beard is covered with frost under the blaze of Evelyn's amorous elation.

René will take away the hat lady's fingers forever in the pockets of his old overcoat. And Evelyn's heart, like a ball of yarn, will tumble out of her chest, will roll and roll, be brave, onto the path of his lips, will roll, kiss me, will roll under a mist of saliva, is that what love is, tell me, it will roll and roll all the way to the starry Provençal night.

13

Cap Tourmente, 29 October 1945

Evie,

You tell me that the untamed hills of Las Vegas fascinate you. And that the desert is like a prayer. You tell me that your little inn at Lake Mead is a haven where you're resting from New York and from our love, which has stolen, taken, hidden everything from us over the past months—your drawing, my painting, our days and our nights, our bodies and our minds.

Rest there, my lady of the hats, rest from me and from our love.

You tell me that you have to stay in Nevada for at least six weeks to get your divorce. Do what you must, my blessed one, my desert angel. And rest yourself from me. From my shoulders, dead in your arms, and from my lips, still swollen from our kisses.

As for me, I am trying to catch hold of the wind off the St. Lawrence at Cap Tourmente, still packed with snow geese just now, where I've set up my easel and my frugal life. I try to capture the slight breeze, you know that breeze, the thin shiver the geese make as they fly away above the capes and the small ports. I try to take hold of the faint wind that's as insubstantial as a dream, try to pour it into the alluvium of my paintings.

I am at the river's edge where my heart is sailing in the stern of our wretched history. I see boats, Evie, small ones, big ones, boats made of bark and of wood, with sails and with motors, old tubs, Evie, and the river ships from Île aux Coudres, schooners and tugs, that ply the shore past our little expressions of happiness and past our terrible wounds, sailing on the route of our inadequacies and our oh-so-generous intentions.

I see Hurons and Montagnais, sons of iron and of the blue northern suns, daughters of sweet corn and porcupines, taken by force from their dense forests to travel up the St. Lawrence and adorn the courts of French kings.

I see the fishermen of our coasts, their fingers sliced by the lines that bring in the fish. And the blood from their fingers spurting onto the cod.

I see my father on skis, racing crazily across the ice on the bay at Pointe-aux-Outardes, which cracks behind him as he goes, avoiding chaos at every glide of those thin boards, a solitary man given over to the eternity of a continent of ice that has just broken away in the wind from the west. And all those men slouched in the streetcars travelling along Notre-Dame Street towards the elevators in the port of Montreal, feeding them with the rhythm of the grain from dawn till night, in the powerful smells of fresh water and of dead sturgeon in the St. Lawrence.

I see those thousands of French Canadians going up another river, a long column of carts crossing the infinite plains, spreading out like termites across endless, flat, mendacious lands. They were going to settle the Canadian west, Evie. In hay wagons. My father was one of them. Set off one day with two children in his cart. Came back ten years later but thirty years older, with eight more children piled into the same cart. A truckload of children. Before he died, he wanted to see his river again, the first river of his days, the river made of water and rushes, the St. Lawrence.

I see those who drowned in that river, Evie, who never came back from their heroic and suicidal log-driving at the mouths of smaller rivers. And all those people of dark waters who don't know how to swim. Nor do their parents. Or their children. Who only know how to drown, Evie. And our soldiers, swallowed up in the blood that surged from the beaches of Normandy and all the way here. The news from Europe is finally good. But dear God, so many drowned and dead!

I wish that I could knead the soul of the St. Lawrence and roll it out on my canvases, an unforgettable paste of boats and the drowned, of snow geese and hay wagons.

I wish I knew how to paint that genesis of water, that genetics of the river flowing in the veins of our men, that complicity of wind and memories and lakes. And by remaking the bed of memory, to remake that of painting, too.

You will come here and see the light from that river, Evelyn. I'll bring you. Light that is impossibly grandiose, impossible to lay down on canvas. Too huge. Like an over-abundance of space for a period of history that's too brief. Impossible. Unless one is a genius. I wish I had that genius: can you understand?

I struggle, exhaust myself, start over time after time until I tear the skin from my fingers, I peel my scabs one by one, doing everything anew, starting everything over, again and always, fluvium rasum, *I no longer sleep, enslaved by my colours, obsessed by the longing to offer that light, Evie, to dazzle, to dazzle you, the blinding luminescence of the day, unfathomable in its lava-like clarity.*

You and your people in the Town of Mount Royal know nothing or practically nothing about that light. Save a few of you who summer at Métis Beach across from here, on the other shore. A few hundred of you who have dared to travel east, past the city of Quebec, a few hundred who stop up your front doorsteps and barricade your villas when autumn comes back to the River, followed by the beastly cold, while we return to our henhouses and our poaching.

Do you sometimes feel melancholy, Evie? Do you feel something like a pain that goes back in time and now studies itself over time's shoulder? Or like a kind of prior boredom, but we don't know which one? A yawning gap in the heart of history, but we no longer know which history? I'll sing to you "Un Canadien errant," my Evie, the lament that brings tears to everyone here.

> Un Canadien errant, banni de ses foyers
> Parcourait en pleurant des pays étrangers.
> Un jour triste et pensif, assis au bord des flots,
> Au courant fugitif, il adressa ces mots:
> Si tu vois mon pays, mon pays malheureux,
> Va dire à mes amis que je me souviens d'eux.[I]

Take advantage of every second in your desert, Evelyn, my lady of the hats. I'll wait for you as no one has ever waited for anybody or anything. Except perhaps a painter who waits for the wind.

René

14

SHE SITS, LEGS STRETCHED OUT on the gallery of the inn that looks down on Lake Mead, slowly smoking a Player's in a hot desert night where the breeze and the moon are full.

No need to step into the lake to bathe in its water. In the depths of the night she swims in the vast pool open onto Pegasus and Cassiopeia, saying to herself alone that the breeze ought to be edible.

The evening air is more watery than the water. The evening air will be her nighttime bath.

Her youth, she knows, ends here, in this night with its aquarium and cicadas. The cicadas are more night than the night.

Love exists, however, in its fiery vitality. At every moment, Evelyn dies from it.

But this night, she knows, is the last of her vivid youth, because it signs forever the end of her carefree life. Since she herself is feverishly waiting, Evelyn will know that she is awaited and responsible for a joy that must be renewed again and again. Love is a game for grownups. She learned that when Bernard, the dandy, Bernard Leshley, that proud god, knelt down before her, beseeching her, his sobs now silent, not to go.

Annihilated in the sweetness of the night on Lake Mead, she embraces weightlessness and contemplates its tranquillity.

Suddenly, a thing she'd never seen before stood up in the flesh of the moon, something she would never see again: a kangaroo, enormous creature, seeming to inhale from the height of its grandeur and with its cosmic nostrils some mark from the star.

The kangaroo will disappear completely just as it's come, turning the corner of the moon to hurl itself into sidereal space in the same way that Evelyn's youth is in the process of vanishing, turning the corner of freedom to enter into love.

Tomorrow, she leaves to meet René in New York.

Part Two

Hungers

The Years of Symbiosis

15

Where does this uncontrolled appetite for knowledge come from, this unappeasable hunger for lights, for all the lights with their transcendant haloes that have come before them? They're insatiable. Mad. Burlesque. They devour everything that New York possesses by way of museums, operas, theatre, ballet, bookstores.

Evelyn's work is now seen regularly on the covers of *Vogue* and *Cosmopolitan*. She has gone from Lord & Taylor to Bonwit Teller, she's the new star of New York fashion and commands tremendous fees. Agencies fight over her.

She has bought an apartment at the corner of Fifth Avenue and Seventy-first Street that looks down on the Frick Museum, a tiny, peaceful, nearly private place of which she and René have made their home, an annex to their official address: the Frick Museum whose gardens they've looked out on from their living room since they first arrived. They just have to offer their nostrils, hold out an arm, and they can breathe in and touch the old masters' paintings, those whose outlines René had copied from the postcards handed out in the churches of Montreal—the Raphaels, the Della Francescas that were the only artworks to which he, child of the twenties, had access. While Saint-Henri and its three-rooms-eight-children apartments was on its knees for the evening rosary, under the long johns of the frozen workers hung up to dry above the stove. And while men from the North Shore, from the Gaspé, from La Mauricie, raced from one mill to the next, an axe between their teeth and boots cut from potato sacks on their feet.

Hunger. Hunger for other things. Foolish, furious hunger. For everything and for elsewhere.

Evelyn, in the wealthier Town of Mount Royal, hadn't really been exposed to anything but a reproduction of a Turner showing Admiral Nelson's ship routing the French army at Trafalgar that hung prominently in the living room; a stream during the spring break-up taken from an IODE calendar; the Victrola on which her father could play the *William Tell* Overture on Saturday afternoons; the upright piano and the lamps with lace doilies draped over their shades.

These were their only nourishment. Theirs and their fathers'. While Paris was gazing at its new Eiffel Tower and recovering from its World Fair and inaugurating the moving walkway on the left bank of the Seine. These were their only foods. While Colette, Cocteau, Artaud, Picasso reigned supreme, they were building their log houses or were descending with their lunch pails to smash the jaw of their Irish foreman.

Where did that sidereal hunger come from? From want. From bigotry. From the intellectual poverty maintained by a society where there was more future, so they were told, in "walking to Catechism" than in memorizing the alphabet. Where mathematics was learned at the abacus of indulgences granted for sins, venial or mortal. Where the angels, archangels and seraphim cultivated their imaginations rather than Nelligan and Laure Conan, Cendrars and Mallarmé, Joyce and Fitzgerald.

That's where they came from.

They are insatiable. Intent on making up for privation, obstinately creating their own lives and their works of art. They run. From the Metropolitan Museum to Swan Lake to Tosca to Shostakovich, they run like greased lightning. While Evelyn is drawing at Bonwit Teller, René is painting in the apartment. They meet at the end of the day in the Museum of Modern Art on Fifty-third Street. They race again, they're hungry, so hungry, it is beauty that will save them, they run, they run, above all don't turn around, it is art, artistic creation, that will extract them both from their predestination. Don't look back, no more Saint-Henri, no more the Town of Mount Royal. Now it's Rembrandt and Van Dyck, but also Matisse and Bonnard, whose gigantic rumbling has come from Europe to America's shores, who will heal them. They know: vaguely, but they know. And they run. Out of breath. No more family, ever, no more friends, pennants, vigil lights, icicles, no one, never again.

16

Who is prisoner of whom, Evelyn of René or René of Evelyn? The door to 3 East Seventy-first Street is closed to any third person. René painting maniacally from morning till night, refusing any visitor, any invitation. He finds the slightest criticism of his work unbearable, and the slightest questioning infuriates him. "Evie, Evie, can you see the wind, can you see the wind blowing across my canvases? Tell me, Evie, tell me that you can see."

She too works day and night, in the inflamed discovery of a lust for life, for life as she's never lived it before, finally set free of her youth with its starched clothes and carefully done hair. Dior's New Look arrives in America as a shock. The Paris collections land in New York amid the post-war frenzy. She is fascinated.

Though very active outside, spending time with the stars of the fashion world, its studios, photographers, models, tailors and admen, Evelyn is building her prison from this paradox: on leave outside, locked up inside.

Both become reclusive, every day adding a stone to the fortress they erect to protect themselves from the world, every day confirming to themselves once more their determination to escape the snares of their former lives, every day repeating to themselves that it's better to live confined than abused.

She constantly goes into raptures over René's paintings. Her admiration of him and of his work is absolute. And though she is solicited, wealthy, admired, she tells herself over and over that it's he who is her salvation, day after day, he who stimulates her, makes her surpass herself and surpass her destiny, forever inscribed in the sky, of apprentice hatmaker at Eaton's. They owe everything to art and she owes everything to René. Between them has settled in, ever so surreptitiously, ever so furtively, a kind of master-pupil relationship from which neither one can break away. Their life has become their jail.

But a jail that still leaves her stunned with happiness at times, when the sun sets over Central Park and they go to see "Starry Night" again, and René, discreetly, takes her hand. Then the love of men and women, their own love, the love of the earth surges like melted stars, nuggets of crushed humanity.

Every time, Evelyn comes away from it breathless. A human hand, trembling and warm, holding hers? He doesn't like to touch her any more than he likes her to touch him. Evelyn has never known anything else, in fact. Such coolness was determined farther back than memory. She who is still waiting for her mother's caress in her little gilded bed in TMR.

He who had never been given a kiss save in a dark organ loft in Saint-Henri, once, just one ecstatic time, by a lord with feet of incense who had sung an unforgettable "Panis Angelicus," that kiss, more disturbing than a woman's breast gorged with milk. At the time he was thirteen years old.

17

Never satisfied with his paintings, René would grumble about the "too much," too much emphasis, too much pretension, or about the "not enough," not enough movement, not enough burning, or he would grumble about the drabness, or about the mannered, considering his whites to lack brightness or his greens to be too green or his blues excessive. Evelyn would leave him in the morning already furious at his brushes, and in the evening she'd find him with the dregs of a bottle of Coca Cola and some peanuts that had dropped to the floor in their greasy paper, surrounded by sketches still trembling from his angry outbursts. Every time, Evelyn would encourage him to stay on this road that was his and she'd comment on his work, comments she adapted to his mood, but always praising his talent and his tenacity. He sneered at her in silence for admiring his work. The way we sneer at those who love us and whom we don't love. And yet, he loved her. Or so he told himself.

Wearing his old camel-hair coat, he would walk for hours in Central Park, in the heart of the night, groping to find the way to paint the respirations of the world. He took photos, thinking in that way to grasp the keys to the wind, finally captive in his fluttering fingers. With one dry click his flashes pierced holes in the New York night.

But it was a waste of time. He would go back to 3 East Seventy-first Street looking lost, somewhat crazed, he was only going in circles, he thought. It was too well-drawn, too figurative, not bare enough. The wind should not, could not, be more than suggested, evoked, in one spare and simple gust.

Farmhouse that stands resolute under the chimerical assaults of René Marcil, the wind was still desperately unassailable, like the bird of time that we can hear all around us but can't see.

One night, after a performance of *A Midsummer Night's Dream,* René was developing photos in the dark with Evelyn at his side. New York was a dancing sea of lights, an indescribable racket at their window. He slaps her face. "I detest you." Once, twice. "You're just half an artist." Some acid had spilled. They didn't switch on the lights.

In the dimness they could hear nothing but the din from their terror-stricken chests. They stood there frozen in front of the photos flecked with acid that were like bloodstains on a sheet.

Of that they never spoke again. Evelyn put it down to her painter-husband's despondency.

That night she didn't notice the broken leg of the little tame bird, a canary perhaps, which they had been keeping in a cage since they'd moved into 3 East Seventy-first Street, that the next morning, mysteriously, died.

18

23 October 1949

Evie,

It's been four years now that I have been living under your roof, a roof that will never be mine. I can't attach myself to it, any more than to anywhere else in my life. I cannot find either my time or my place. Except beside the Della Francesca in our Frick Museum, where I wish I could become a statue.

Everything resists me. Forms, angles, colours. My fingers, my brushes. At every moment I am struggling against the urge to break everything, including you. How can I make any sense of that, Evie, do you know?

Though you tell me that you have no fears where money is concerned and that you're happy to let me paint without having to earn my daily salt, I can't take any more of this existence.

This Senator McCarthy from Wisconsin, who's beginning to draw big crowds, makes me vomit and I see in New York an ugly, disgusting face that looks too much like mine. What comes to us from Europe, from France, gives me some hope.

I need wind. The vital breath. As the blade of grass needs the breath of the earth. And bullfrogs in ponds need the evening breeze.

Japanese painters say that one must become on the inside that which one aspires to depict outside. I want to be the wind, Evie, fragrant with honeysuckle and wild roses, with the smell of cod and wild pears. Abandoned to the stars like a dog on his back, I want to sniff my life with wide-open nostrils. I want to swallow warblers and gulp down hummingbirds, to digest and then regurgitate them into the wind of my fingers on the canvas. Because birds are the bones of the wind, Evie. And the painter is a poet, like an alluring net.

I am leaving for France. With your money, which is my sustenance and my shame. On an Air France flight that you'll have paid for.

René

19

Leaning on the ship's rail of the *Liberté* in this golden spring of 1950, Evelyn watches as Le Havre comes closer. She crosses the water in the basin of Le Havre, glides across the patina of verdigris waves, her heart pounding when she recognizes the light, the impalpable light of Monet's "Terrasse à Sainte-Adresse" which she has admired for so long in the Metropolitan Museum. She drifts across the white flame of the waves, her body leaning back under the caress of the pale rays, she has come from so far away, from the cold, the skin of her eyes salty like the air, simply, she exults. America, where she has left behind her worldly goods, sold apartment, piano and furniture, is already well behind her. Kneeling in the periwinkle of this day's dawn, she is purely jubilant.

A while ago, at the sight of cliffs sliced with a sabre that ran along the boat, an oppressive question had passed through her: how had men, bare-handed men, been able to climb such a palisade under rockets and bullets, suffocated by the webbing of their kitbags, a light machine-gun across their backs? How, will you tell me, how? It was there, almost within reach, that her mother's two brothers had died, their chests nailed to the rock face, torn apart like two spiders caught in a web of smoking flesh and shrapnel. In the midst of superhuman shouts of mutual encouragement and the death rattle of the dying. It was there that both had died, her young uncles whose clownish behaviour had given her so many laughs. Crucified on the walls of this atrocious shambles.

But the fire of her joy had triumphed over the fire of old bombs. She could do nothing about it, she couldn't contain everything that was making her entire being explode with the anticipated bliss of discovery that awaited her. As for the journey that would bring her to she knew not where, it didn't matter, she was almost touching the end of the world.

The *Liberté* is now in harbour. Far away, children are playing on the shingle beach. Evelyn can see them clearly. They're throwing bits of wood at foolish dogs that under their laughing imprecations, go flying into the sea. A crowd has gathered on the landing stage to greet the travellers. The liner roars, three long rumbles of thunder.

Suddenly, she spots him. René. René Marcil, still so far from her, so tiny there on the beach, a stone among other stones in his old camel-hair coat. Alone, set back from the crowd, at attention before the shimmering Channel.

They melt into one another's arms without a word. And the light of Monet, Dufy, Boudin, and all the lights of the sky and the sea will take them in its milky arms. While a tear will fall, just one, onto René's cheek, as if it doesn't know what to do with itself, dazed to find itself there.

A tear from him to her.

On the beach at Le Havre. Evelyn has just given him the gift of tears—this man who has never wept. And with the gift of tears, the gift of the wind, oh the most minuscule of all the kinds of wind: the one that produces a human tear which spills over from the eyelid and runs onto the cheek.

That same night they are in Paris, embracing in an attic room of a small hotel near Saint-Sulpice. The Seine close by is an old silver teapot turned upside down between Notre-Dame and the Conciergerie. From its spout runs a slender thread of moonlight.

They love one another in that attic room, they adore one another as they never have before. Paris is mint tea, sweet like their endless kisses.

That night, in Evelyn's arms, René tries out his new tears.

20

The room is vast and brimming over with soul. Wooden chairs. Wooden easels. Wooden floors: long boards polished like those in a dance studio. Heavy velvet drapes.

At the back of this maroon and chocolate casket, slightly raised, is a trestle, also wooden, where models pose next to a cast-iron stove with the curves of a tobacco pipe.

Every day, for a ridiculously low price, the Académie Grande Chaumière welcomes into its tanned belly whatever painters show up there. In their day, Modigliani and Soutine came to this den in the heart of Montparnasse. René, faithful among the faithful, arrives every day at first light.

Two floors above, he can hear Coco howling at the moon from his perch like a sick old wolf, Coco, once a model for Matisse, magnificently ugly now and nothing but skin and bones. And two tinned feathers that bend down from his skull like the branches of a weeping willow. Every morning, René can hear the old character repeat, "Ah! How bright the night is, don't you agree?" Coco leaves to go to sleep, high on alcohol and boys in petticoats.

As soon as the door to the Académie is shut and the fire started in the stove, the ceremony can begin.

The model, a young man or young woman, undresses, tossing the clothes in a ball into a corner of the trestle. How to explain the shyness that everyone seems to share at watching these young people while they strip, when the group will have no scruples about their posing, about scrutinizing the model from every angle?

As if the flesh of the men and the women who are stripping, reduced to its absurd humanity by these desperately prosaic movements, were more intimidating than the stark naked body exhibited in all its glory.

Now the model gets into position before the easels lined up as in an orchestra pit.

René observes at length. Then he launches into a kind of gesticulation in the air, movements at first angular and rather abrupt, then more and more sweeping, round, casual, until he seems to be beating time for an andante. Then he slashes his blank paper, his quick, nearly panicky movements composing first a head, then a torso, spatters of body in the cesspool of an engraving. Most important: not to lose his vision which in a second will have disappeared.

He will draw like that, stacks of sheets of paper, day after day, until evening. Turning from rage to resignation, from inhibiting doubt to conscientious audacity.

How many talents have broken their teeth in this studio on rue Grande Chaumière? How many dreams burst like old balloons? Quests for water, for winds, for dust, disappointed, flown away, deceived? Then outbursts of impatience and outcries at the unfairness of fate? Of exasperation in the face of refusals, by gallery owners, museums, critics? How many lives washed up on the reefs of lack of recognition or, quite simply, of genius? *You need to have the gift, without it, it will break your heart.*[2]

When the Mass has been said and René emerges from his buried world and finally sticks his head out, the sun is a vast crimson eye that drops into the plane trees.

Down! But the beast won't hear of it. Paris is rousing itself for the night.

While Coco is starting his day.

21

Evelyn delights in the raging beast, travelling excitedly through its entrails to its very heart. Seated on the great Saurian, Amazon-style, she floats from the Sainte-Chapelle to the Orangerie to the Eiffel Tower, rolling out before her aesthetic shocks, architectural emotions, taking hold of splendours with her windswept hand.

Notre-Dame seen from the Pont d'Austerlitz seems like a pachyderm squatting on its hind legs, she thinks. The first time Evelyn went inside, there was a seismic shock, quite unexpected, when the organist started playing Couperin. At once she started to cry and couldn't stop. Oddly enough, she thought about her mother, oddly enough because she had convinced herself that her mother no longer existed or, if she did, that she, Evelyn Rowat, had been able to forget her.

From Notre-Dame to Montmartre to Saint-Germain, the young woman had all the time in the world and a fortune before her, living on her assets and having her companion benefit from them, too, without counting. "When there's no more there'll be something else."

Never, no matter where she is, will she stop sending money to René.

22

I SEE HER, posing for René in the apartment on rue Séguier, leaning against the Quai des Grands Augustins, docile, careful not to move a muscle before the painter who's as cantankerous as an old bear. When she moves even slightly, after endless minutes of holding her breath and without the slightest hint of relaxation, he yells. She settles back then without a word and resumes her frozen posture, making herself again mineral, congealed inside her plaster skin, trying to reduce the pulse of her heart, which beats all the harder when she wants to bury it. Like a fit of giggles.

Prisoner of her painter-companion's gaze for nights at a time, in a prison whose bars are made of René's grimace and his pained features. She is sometimes the prey chained to its predator, sometimes the lamb of the loving shepherd, she herself also in love. Shackled but fascinated. Captive captivated. While René's tormented wife, her rage repressed, wants to flee her chains, the model of Marcil the painter cries out for more, in love with her shackles.

A peculiar couple, well-matched by the mediation of the easel, but ill-matched by their love alone. A peculiar couple, to whom the danger of the canvas matters more than anything else.

René tries to find the light that haloes Evelyn's nude body, tries to find the shadows that she belongs to, brighter than the day, milky-white brightness that flows down her torso. A thousand times he cuts out her profile and cuts it out again, carving the curve of her face or her hip.

Now dawn appears on the Quai des Grands Augustins. The mud of the painter's colours mixes with the mud of sweating bodies, tangle of hair and paintbrushes, hodgepodge of hair and hairbrushes, desire in the body fitted into the desire in the painter's work. Mouths that drink in the pigments on the canvas, mouths of your hands salivating and dripping, they are hungry, so hungry, lay down on me your colours, half-starved strollers in the snowy clearings, lovers whose feet are cold, draw me, I beg you, they call, call, hollow cries, raving mad as the prayers of convicted prisoners, I beg you, pour onto our skins destitution and our uncommon souls, they're hungry, so very hungry.

And love one another to death in the soothing dawn.

23

Evelyn had furnished elegantly the apartment on rue Séguier thanks to the auction sales at the Hôtel Drouot. She had made of it a haven of work and peace with, at its heart, a vast room with brick walls and big windows that served as a studio for her painter-husband from where he could glimpse the spire of the Sainte-Chapelle, rising into the sky of Paris like a javelin.

One day, overjoyed and thinking she had finally found a place where René would enjoy living for a long time, she announced to him that she'd just purchased the lease for 14 rue Séguier, a nine-year lease, for the preposterous sum of five thousand dollars. Afterwards, it would cost them just two hundred dollars in annual, nearly insignificant rent.

René's only acknowledgement was to hurl a can of paint at the mirror, livid. And without further ado disappeared into the night and didn't come back until dawn. She was silent, dumbfounded. Paralyzed.

Unbelievable yet true, the next day Evelyn put up for sale the lease that she'd just concluded. And started to pack her bags. It was February, 1954.

René wanted to go home to Montreal, to Cap Tourmente, to Pointe-aux-Outardes, home to America. He missed

America, its rough-hewn inhabitants, their insufficiently civilized work and lives, the blue lips of frosty roads.

The old stones of Paris, though he regarded them as an exquisite part of the beauty of the world, had all at once become the stuff of his regrets. And in the forest of Saint-Germain-en-Laye where he sometimes went walking, and in all the forests of old France—picked over, swept, dusted, flawless rows of plane trees and oaks, their gleaming undergrowth, and all its primped and polished gardens—he now felt only a knot of nostalgia. All that perfection made his head ache.

What he missed was the wild, the undomesticated. Dark woods in disorderly regrowth. Land left fallow, stumps offered like roadside crosses. All that robust and unaffected life created, finally, an elegant way of being. And the tall frozen rushes on the St. Lawrence across from Verchères and Berthier and Donnacona. And the untouched skies, so limpid they seem endless, seem already to stand out from the infinity of the cosmos.

What he missed—how to put it?—was something rickety, something like the playful recklessness of one who has not suffered from great wars, from pogroms and the Inquisition, only from climates of indescribable bleakness. And from the rapacity of man for man, though such rapacity is shared equally everywhere on the globe. Bits and pieces of souls and bodies let loose in the voracious ecstasy of respite after the inordinate elements and the blackest misery have been vanquished.

What he missed were city backyards shrieking with children, the mismatched colours and materials of the cladding on houses, toothless shapes, erratically bulging reliefs, the somewhat rustic discord. What he missed was the variety of relaxation, the pretentious offhandedness outside the churches, the skipped syllables and guttural laughter of his peers on that side of the Atlantic, something unconstrained, not held back, something unorganized. What he missed was the virginity of the New World.

René Marcil was pining for his native land.

Where his painting, he thought, when all's said and done, would be better understood.

24

POINTE-AUX-OUTARDES, WINTER 1956

Evie,

You tell me that New York is buried in snow and that your eyes stayed behind on rue Séguier. That you sometimes make a kind of telescope from your two hands, shrinking your field of vision, reducing it to the single dimension of a few square metres of the rippling Hudson River, a particle of the Hudson's skin beneath the clouds. So you imagine, you firmly believe, that it's the Seine that is shimmering between your curled palms. You close your eyes and you see, can almost touch, the Pont Mirabeau, the towers of Notre-Dame and the slender tip of the Vert Galant, from where you could lean over and wash your hair.

From your snowy New York where you dream of Paris, you can see me standing in my own Laurentian storm, one man standing on the farthest rock on Pointe-aux-Outardes where, centuries ago, I left behind my father on his thin skis. You can see me impaled on my easel in the blizzard, also dreaming of an elsewhere. But your elsewhere is accessible. Mine is not.

Where do I have to go, Evie?

I had thought that the winds from the ice floe, or those that embrace the leafless northern trees like snakes biting their tails, that those winds would brighten my horizon, that I would lose myself there the better to find myself, like the little airplane on skis I caught a glimpse of the other day, trying to find the trail in the gusting winds and the intense snow, started over once, twice, three times, trying to find the clear current, searching the stagnant air for a second piece of evidence that would let him touch down. Ah, how I'd have liked to be that pilot who was able to find his way in the white bush land between the emergency lights on either side of the corridor, who was able to restore the earth and the sky from their undifferentiated magma.

I thought that out of the mess in which I find myself and from where I am writing to you now, fitted into my box of colours, there would develop at last the birth of the day.

But mediocrity is slowly swallowing me, Evie. Salt-marsh worker of misfortune, I'm afraid of the spring that's on its way, the season of sinking into the new mud on the ground. I watch it coming with dread.

Will I annoy you, Evie, scandalize you even, if I tell you that I too miss the rancio of France and its clemency, Evie, a clemency that at this moment strikes me as infinite, that of the mint cordials on café terraces, of the radishes in bunches on the merchants' stalls and of the oblique light from which angels fall? And if I tell you that soon I will head for the blossoming almond trees and the narcissi that are starting to show their noses in Bonnard's hills far to the south? Will it be hard for you if I add: will you come there and meet me, Evie?

I will come via New York where you were kind enough to show some of my paintings to the Van Diemen-Lilienfeld Gallery. If you sell one I'll finally be able to break my dependence on the money you send me. Maybe I'll even be able to pay back part of what I owe you.

Now I'll go back to my blizzard, dreaming of the bluish breezes of Provence.

René

25

EVELYN HAD DONE SOMETHING REMARKABLE, nearly impossible in fact, when the famous Van Diemen-Lilienfeld Gallery on Fifty-seventh Street, known for discovering talented artists, had opened its door to her because of her determination, her skill at handling people and the power of her convictions.

She believed that her husband's talent was exceptional and, armed with his portfolio, had managed to persuade Karl Lilienfeld that it would be fitting to devote an exhibition to the painter René Marcil.

Evelyn had also shown him a letter from the Guggenheim Museum whose director said that he'd been overwhelmed by one of René's paintings, "Still Life with Red and Green Apples," which he'd painted some years earlier, on rue Séguier. And for which she herself felt a particular affection. At the time, though, the painter had neglected to respond to the explicit request of Sweeney, the director, who had written, "I was struck by the large still life which you very kindly left at the Museum for our viewing. I trust in the course of the coming summer you may consider letting us see further subsequent examples of your work."

Pursuing her own electrifying career in the New York fashion world, Evelyn had taken the resounding *yes* of the

Van Diemen-Lilienfeld Gallery as a personal victory added to a record already marked with a series of successes.

And so Evelyn was seeing the fulfillment of what she imagined was the dream of any person who was in love with another: to bring him the moon on a silver platter. That was, she thought, one of the most dazzling tasks that love could accomplish, one that few are so fortunate as to experience. The international career of the painter René Marcil had been launched. The canvases would be hung in May. But the moon had already been taken down.

With no company but her own, she had savoured that grace by sipping a few drops of Lagavulin. She had raised a glass of the amber nectar come directly from the salt marshes of Scotland to René's success. And to what had to be called their love, that strangeness which was still alive, almost in spite of them.

And that night, in front of a New York studded with the lights from thousands of small boats anchored close to the cliffs of the Empire State Building, she had written these words, just for herself, that bore the title *Lagavulin.*

> *Lagavulin my misty love, I nestle between your iodine breasts, take me, take me to the salt of your lips, Lagavulin, my smoky tenderness, take me to the ocean's depths, inhale me all the way to the sweetness of the bottom of the sea, the sea that I love infinitely more than the heights of humanity where the desert is inscribed. Do you know that, Lagavulin? Which desert is more arid—land or human?*
>
> *Lagavulin, the little yellow flower that I offered you, no, thank you, I have no need of anything, I have everything if I have your love and my firebird dreams*

above the city's lights. Lagavulin, tonight the Empire State Building is steeping in my smokeless glass. No, thank you, I have no need of anything.

So slow, Lagavulin. I wanted to tell you it's been so long since I've drunk such a nostalgic potion. I like nostalgia, Lagavulin, can you understand that? You were my golden wheat, for all those months you were the only portion of myself that would let me stretch out. Strange, but you were my only soul during that whole winter. And when it snowed onto my breast it was you who covered it with a fine feathering of white kisses.

White kisses and green apples, Lagavulin, you were my winter soul, my Lagavulin winter, white kisses and red apples.

26

New York, late May, 1956. René had taken barely enough time to tour the gallery and had only caught a glimpse of his paintings, exhibited in an inspiring and quiet setting. He ordered the exhibition to be taken down at once, without another word.

Then he turned around and walked away.

A few days later, Evelyn received a cable from Karl Lilienfeld. "I take note of the decision of your husband to withdraw his paintings. I look forward to your visit to make the necessary arrangements. With my kindest regards."

It was the only exhibition of the work of René Marcil during his lifetime. It lasted for two and a half days.

Part Three

The Consolation of Freedom

The Years of Instability

27

CABRIÈRES D'AIGUES. FEBRUARY, 1964. First glimmers of daylight, the line of trees is beginning to stand out against the jet-black horizon. One part of Evelyn is reassured, her daytime energy is restored. These southern early mornings when nothing seems familiar have something awe-inspiring about them. Unfamiliar nature, limestone and pebbles, where rosemary and shadberry flower in winter, while red-legged partridges haunt the groves of oaks and great horned owls haunt the nights. Incongruous world, world upside-down. Perfumes new and haunting: lavender, thyme, sage. Everywhere, brushwood fires streak the sky, offering an arm to the clouds. Caught in this exhilaration of fragrance, Evelyn murmurs to herself that if she weren't made of flesh she would be made of scents like those.

The steam from her coffee drifts onto the window as condensation, as if the distance between herself and the world were beading on the glass. It's she who is boiling inside, while outside it's still raw.

In recent years, she had renewed her ties with the fragility of solitude. When everything, absolutely all the beauty and the ugliness of existence, can only be grasped, can only be assessed beginning with oneself and oneself only. When dialogue can be initiated from one's own things without emphasis, the blaze of speech and sharing with a loved one.

Patiently, she'd got used to the idea that introducing herself to the world as a solo rather than a duet was riskier, but also simpler. That recklessness suited her. She had convinced herself that freedom, real freedom, the kind that no one ever talks about in a world where not being one of a pair is like a physical handicap, a partial paralysis of the being, that it was the price of freedom pure and simple. She had finally come to enjoy this pitiless work, in spite of her early tears and initial reluctance. Learning how to live alone, she had invented a clever equilibrium for herself in the whirlwind of a flourishing artistic career.

The recent reunion with René had made official the break with herself, creating the kind of difficult equilibrium that's won after a hard fight. Everything was, in a sense, to be started from square one. To fit herself to herself again, but from now on and once again, one more time assenting to it completely.

This fragrant Provence morning takes her back to all that. The sound and the fury of her life in New York continue to move in her even though the notes fell silent a moment ago.

The sky had turned pale, was now a bluish mauve. Evelyn can distinguish the stones in the low wall that lines the house where she lives with René, and the shrubs that carpet the foot of Mount Luberon. And now, a few metres away, she notices in the lingering half-light an enormous snow-white mass. A horse, chewing flowers and herbs.

Huddled over her steaming coffee, Evelyn sees on the animal's right flank, facing the Gorges de Verdon, a huge pink sun that's rising like a diamond-studded peony. And on its left flank, facing the Dentelles de Montmirail, an ivory crescent moon. Evelyn's heart was cut in two down the middle. Each half, like the two parts of herself, rolled in the morning purity. Evelyn gathered them up. Doubting that she would ever be able to stick them together again.

Now the day was settling in by sections and slabs as if in a mouth with teeth of gold. Narcissi were opening their throats to greet their mouthful of light. Under the authority of hunters, packs of dogs were howling on the trail of some prey or other. Birds whose chirping Evelyn had never heard before were bickering or murmuring sweet nothings, she didn't know which.

The sun was emerging now against the light on the blonde skin of the meadows and on that, spotlessly white, of the horse. While behind, to the south, Mont Sainte-Victoire, an enormous liner caught in the blaze of the rising sun, its hull stretching all the way to Africa, or so Evelyn imagined the confines of the world on that morning. Mont Sainte-Victoire, which she'd admired so often in catalogues and on posters and had seen with her own eyes at the Philadelphia Museum of Art, with René: now she had become its dumbfounded near-neighbour. Slightly incredulous.

Here, the sublime was not in the grandiosity of the sea nor the excess of high mountains, Evelyn thought. No. Here, the sublime dwelled in the harmony of the elements. Horizontality and verticality reconciled at last. Vines, hills, brooks and streams, long cypresses and dwarf olive trees shading from the darkest to the most translucent shadows—all these registers tenderly arranged on the landscape like kisses on a broad face, a concentrate of sweetness fallen onto the earth.

And down there, guessed-at, sensed, the Mediterranean wreathed in mystery, the fine points of all things and of life itself.

Offered heart of the splendour that was tracing its reassuring way in the body and in the mind of the new arrival, whom the sun, now well along the way to the height of its glory, was spattering.

28

May, 1966. Crouching on the hill, René was painting on its luminous slope, his fingers soaked in ochre pigments, his beard too tinted with the mineral colouring. Morning till night, he could often be seen moving in a strange ballet, his body sloping towards the ground, shoulders grazing the large blank sheet of paper laid out in front of him, spreading on it colours and glazes, glairing it with the mucous membranes of limestone and sandstone taken from the very earth on which he was expending so much energy, on his knees, gorging it with the rosy green of the tiered landscape that went all the way down to the Mediterranean.

He spread his orange-yellow, his reds and rusts onto the microcosm of paper, trying to leave the field of representative painting. Now he wanted not to represent the world, but to evoke it. If he did that, maybe the wind would no longer slip away from his attempts to depict it.

He would sit there all day next to a yellow narcissus and, holding his breath and holding back his painter's hand, he would *adore it slowly,*[3] until he'd caught the trembling of its corolla opening and closing in the patient composition of the painting. He would sketch only the trembling.

He would try to paint the aroma of the thyme that emerges from the yawning earth at the mauve hour. He would sketch only its aroma.

With his palette he would try to find the demented sky of Van Gogh's "Starry Night" that had sent him and Evelyn into raptures years ago at New York's Museum of Modern Art. This he would do not by plagiarizing the master but by focussing his attention on the flesh of the night above the *mas* where they were staying. Watching.

With his palette he would try again to find the stunning back country in the "Still Life with Candlestick Against a Blue Background," by Nicolas de Stael. Blue so penetrating, more naked than a face, perhaps the blue of the sea where Stael would take flight like a bird some weeks later, after he'd jumped out the window of his studio, a genius defenestrated on the ramparts of Antibes and on his doorstep. In full glory. He was forty-one years old.

But René's fortune had led him, mauled him, elsewhere and otherwise: to an insignificant destiny on the hills of Cabrières d'Aigues from where all he could see was the tip of his own nose stuck in a rotten childhood. Perched on his purple hill he'd done nothing but dawdle, he thought. Land of waters dead and buried, that he was struggling with his work to exhume.

He saw again the scene with Evelyn the other night.

She was repeating some words in French, a few new words that she was desperately trying to pronounce without an accent, laughing at herself and at her phonetically erring ways. He'd hurled himself at her and slapped her. "I hate you." He'd said it in English, he who had always spoken to her only in French.

Saint-Henri was catching up to him, like a buzzing in the ear that won't go away, that muffles the sounds of the world, confirming him in his sealed universe, a foul-smelling oyster in its closed shell.

29

It's hot. The sea is comfortable for bathing and for drinking, Evelyn has been swimming for some time now. She has left her clothes on the shore at Les Saintes-Maries, next to a still-sealed letter from Cabrières. She has swum out a long way.

In the cove where she is playing in the waves, the sea is like a lake. She's alone. And naked. Cleansing both body and soul. The sparkling water makes her already weeping eyes shed their tears, going back to an old story that she'd swept under the carpet of the years and that she'd thought had decomposed in the accumulated strata of oblivion.

It had happened around fifteen years ago, in Paris. She'd accompanied René to the Vert Galant. He was going there to draw, as he so often did. A sudden torrential rain forced them to flee their quiet place. They'd run in the rain to their apartment on rue Séguier, going inside chilled to the marrow and soaked to the bones.

That night, Evelyn had taken an endless, hot and perfumed bath. She was three months pregnant.

And then everything is confused. The water in her womb bursts into the water in the tub. She cries out. René comes running. She sees him again lifting her cautiously, his arms wet with her blood, dragging her out of the enamelled basin. Pieces of flesh were floating in the water. She sees him again calling for an ambulance. Then she hears him say, with precise and poisonous calm, "If you hadn't got rid of it I'd have punched you in the belly till you did."

Now, in the cove, she is washing away her old sorrow that's been silted up with silence. How could she, over all those years, tell herself and make herself believe that René had been right? That a baby was the last thing they needed at the time?

In the current that comes from the east, she swims among urchins and rockfish, sinking into the pools, former valleys now submerged, brushing against meadows of seaweed.

Had she needed so badly to depend on someone *to be able finally to know the consolation of freedom*?[4] What did she need to atone for so badly?

She slips across jellyfish, glides over moray eels, watery giddiness for which she's insatiable.

All at once a dense school of multicoloured fish, a rain of stars shooting up from the abyssal zone, like thousands and thousands of mad birds spinning as if they were a single wing, little mad fish, the capelins of her childhood—one day her father had taken her and her sister to see the capelins sweep onto the beach under the full moon in May. Capelins glittering in the moonlight, loaded by the shovelful into the back of the truck, there were that many, no longer than a hand, small mad fish in every colour, spade, heart, diamond, club, wriggling in the shovel, ace, king, queen, jack, suddenly, in the middle of the mad dance that brushes her cheeks and slips between her legs, appears the face of her mother, "Mother ... No!", where nothing moves, nothing, only a slight quivering of her chin, "Mother ... no, no, no!" Evelyn thrashes the water with her arms and legs as hard as she can, she shakes herself, struggles, a black crab wants to bite her eyes, she resists.

When she resurfaces, out of breath, she inhales so deeply she sees stars.

The cove at Les Saintes-Maries is a screen of white light with a mauve ray darting from it.

30

CABRIÈRES, 13 MAY 1966

Evie, my Evie,

Does the wind only exist because we hear it? Is the wind, the vicious wind, an abstract notion, like whiteness? And Mont Sainte-Victoire: is it more beautiful for being painted by Cézanne?

And love, Evie, is it an idle fancy that slips between our fingers and drops us constantly?

We work in the dark,

Like rats, Evie, like rats we dig the inextricable channels of our nights, we excavate with our teeth, we eat from every plate that can make us love and experience ecstasy, but we know neither how to love nor how to experience that ecstasy. We get rid of weeds, of rocks, but instead of potatoes, stones grow, and we go back to using our sticks and spades; we fish, we jig, but instead of plump codfish we pull out sea toads, and we pick up our gear and our nets; we grope our way, glassy-eyed, into the storm and the dark, we give birth in the snow, and the forceps smash our skulls, but we move on, we continue to move on.

we do what we can,

My canvas is my keyboard, Evie, you know that old joke about Beethoven ... It's said that he was so deaf he sometimes thought he was a painter rather than a musician. My paints are my notes, mere notes in the continuum of the human melody. Inspiration is the inconsolable part of memory between the fingers of the page, the note, the charcoal, the dance step, or between the fingers of Vladimir Horowitz, my personal god, Evie, whom I heard just now on my radio, playing his sublime "Reverie" from the middle of Schumann's Scenes from Childhood, *one of his favourite encore pieces at recitals, the one that puts sobs in the audience, that extremely poignant "Reverie" through which the infinite journey is pursued, the audience is on its feet, Evie, they want more of the "Reverie," they don't want to leave because leaving would seem like extinguishing the sun itself and disconnecting the earth. And just as we reconstruct all of childhood from an odour, we reconstruct the history of the world from a note on the piano or a spot of acrylic on a sheet,*

we give what we have,

melancholy is our daily duty, Evie, on the trembling wings of loops that loop and loop again, over and over.

our doubt is our passion, and passion is our task. The rest is the madness of art.[5]

Work lamp lighted on the hill, just one, I go on, Evie, I continue, I don't let go, desperately ecstatic, in the light of the work lamp on the hill, a man is crying. Because of beauty. And shame. Stardust but relentlessly present. Like a rat, Evie, like a rat.

Is Mont Sainte-Victoire more beautiful for being painted by Cézanne, tell me? And love, Evie, love?

You ran away to Les Saintes-Maries-de-la-Mer. You ran away from my violence and my indignity. Still, try to keep a little bit of me under your headgear, my lady of the hats.

René

31

She had shredded René's letter into a thousand pieces of confetti that flew away in the wind of Les Saintes-Maries. Unread.

The sky had taken on the colour of coral. Evelyn sang as she rocked herself in the trembling of the little waves. She'd been in the sea for hours, her skin fissured from swimming for so long, the old waters of her womb dissolved in those of Les Saintes-Maries.

And the Maries as witnesses suited her just fine. It was in front of them all gathered together that she swore she would leave René, this time for good. Before them: Mary Jacobé, sister of the Virgin, Marie Salomé, mother of James and John, and little Marie-de-la-Mer whom she'd caught sight of in a watery dream, above the rippling of the waves. Little Mary-of-the-Sea whom she embraced for a long moment, a slender silhouette that might perhaps be fifteen years old, which she held against the full length of her breasts.

When the sun had disappeared behind the Église des Saintes-Maries, Evelyn picked up her clothes on the beach.

It seemed to her then that she had three skins: the inner one, that was warm and brimming with sunlight, that she'd cooled down by swimming endlessly in the cove; the outer one, chapped, icy, nearly blue, that was dying for sun but that consented to the evening; and the third, coated with steaming condensation like a skin made of air, a halo of epidermis through which she could see the horizon turning blue.

The night would be clear.

Part Four

Highway

The Years of Separation

32

MARCH, 1973. In its very abundance, New York this morning is nothing but a vast emptiness, a jumble of small sanctioned urgencies. Strange reversal: she feels that of the two of them, it's she who has been abandoned, though it was she who initiated the separation. René writes to her often from London, where he's living now. She dreads his letters, they're at once soothing and stinging, while at the same time she clamours for them, with the persistent feeling that she is walking by herself and has been duped. New York is a den of small sanctioned urgencies that ultimately create a great compliant violence.

It's a lover built like Spencer Tracy, with the manners of a gentleman, or an engaging wild-eyed oddball who leaves his glasses in the fridge, or someone naturally taciturn who clamours for words of love that he can't make to her, perched on one of the posts of a four-poster bed and drunk. Or a tall and affectionate redhead who recites poems to her, his lips fringed with white from her womb, or a crab fisherman who decrees between two acts of love that he prefers the sea, it's less demanding and more faithful, or a cannabis user, a long lean body with prominent ribs, who sows her surrounded by his blue smoke. Small sanctioned urgencies.

Strange, when they leave in the morning she wants to wash everything, to bleach everything, sheets and comforters, to scour, scrub, throw out the ashtrays along with the ashes, is that the new freedom granted by hormones now available from any good pharmacy on the Lower East Side? When they finally leave she wants just one thing: to eradicate all signs of them under an endless shower, to soap her skin, cream it, purge it.

On those mornings, after all the sweatiness of love and alcohol, what she needs in a sense is to wolf down something solid, a sandwich thick with pastrami, while she sits in a booth at Johnny's Delicatessen, the waitress cleaning the bottles of ketchup in front of her boss, whose hair is as greasy as the fries served to his customers, she needs to prove her own innocence—she, Evelyn Rowat Marcil, the flourishing fashion illustrator whose drawings are on the covers of *Vogue* and *Cosmopolitan*, needs to purify herself—with dills and coleslaw.

On those mornings, the mustard in the pastrami sandwich is like the little patch of blue in her father's riddle that can sweep away all the grey from the sky of the Italian, the Englishman and the Pole.

One night, one night only, Evelyn presses her lips against a woman's. They surge together in the crucible of their effervescent bodies. While listening to Janis and drinking Chivas. "Their skin is too soft and their thighs are too flabby," is how she sums up the experiment to Peggie, one of her models, the next day.

Incidentally, how can they do it? All those Peggies, Rebeccas, Rosies who tell her continuously about their frenzied loves, about their bedroom discoveries, until then unimaginable, with men, women, dogs, cats, anything that moves, involving three, four, ten individuals all together?

How do they do it? Those who set ablaze the plumber walking past her window or the pizza delivery boy to whom they open the door naked? How do they do it, those women who're fired up by a Russian or a Negro penis that forces them against a brick wall in a dark alley?

One day, to shut them up, Evelyn invented for herself an inordinate love for Kenneth Langford, a wealthy New York doctor who was able, so she said, to love her like a god. For once, the women were stunned. And finally shut up.

But on this March morning, the sun shining on New York was as dry as a shrivelled membrane. As desire without a prayer. Evelyn, who'd eaten her fill of pastrami, went home to wait for the mailman. Home, with its stench of Javex and cold cream.

To wait, time and again for an envelope to land in her mailbox, an envelope with an English postage stamp.

33

London, 3 November 1973

I've been rooming at Mrs. Shaw's for a few months now. On Brecknock Road, in Islington. In an atmosphere of linen lace with embroidered designs that lie on nests of tables, beneath the crucifix that she's adorned with plastic flowers and a big red heart. Inside the crucifix is an ancient baptismal candle, the one that presided over the baptism of Deirdre, her beloved daughter, nearly forty-eight years ago. Mrs. Shaw took it down from the wall where it has hung for ages and showed me the yellow wax candle-holder fitted into the beechwood cross from which she also pulled a lock of Deirdre's hair, the girl having died of meningitis at the age of four.

We've just had a long chat, she and I, as we often do over tea with lemon at the end of the afternoon. Her kitchen resembles her flowered apron, the camphorated odours of ladies' occupations, perfumes from cookie tins recycled for storing sugar and flour. Mrs. Shaw's home is a touching blend of doll's house and old folks' home. Trinkets collected over a lifetime, clocks everywhere, to count, to compute, perhaps to contain the time that's left.

We chatter, not about this and that but about anything at all. Everything that has happened in her life, slight, no matter how slight, without making a sound. Everything that is trying to compose my own. She never asks a question: Where am I from? Where am I going? Never! With great tact she'll sometimes suggest to this old grump that he change his shirt or take a shower. That's all.

I sometimes invite Mrs. Shaw to look at my paintings in this Hansel-and-Gretel-sized room that I rent from her. Next to the kitchen. My latest pictures still blazing in the dull Islington light. She'll linger in front of some, questioning, frowning. At times, moving her lips as if they were winking, she'll come out with a "Good!" which reassures me; in fact, to tell the truth, I need it. But when she utters a loud "Very good!" can you believe me, Evie, if I tell you that Mrs. Shaw, with her curls and her lace, gives me wings?

Everything is straightforward, you might say, with Mrs. Shaw. So modest, so pathetic. And the four o'clock tea with lemon and a bit of sugar melts onto my heart along with her little cakes.

Some days, I like to take the bus that hurtles down the sloping streets all the way to Victoria Station, my feet resting on the second-storey railing of these red comets with portholes and ticket taker as it plunges towards the Thames. There, I am at ease. I forget about painting and my pictures, I forget the time, which is sliding towards evening, I forget the medicinal instructions of Dr. Petit of the French Clinic who is treating me for "schizophrenic episodes." When I'm there, I forget who I am.

Then, at nightfall, I go back to Mrs. Shaw's. And the scent of her melon jam that's been simmering all afternoon consoles me for everything, absolutely everything.

Other days, I'll stroll among the paths of Hyde Park Cemetery, near Mrs. Shaw's house. And do you know where I stop for a long while every time, Evelyn? You'll never guess ... at the grave of Karl Marx. He who shook up the earth all the way to heaven, taking it off its axis for decades and taking millions of men, women and children with him, there he is in a small patch of that same earth where burrs and dandelions have sprung up. And I think that great destinies could sometimes use Mrs. Shaw's melon jam.

I walk in London, a rather lanky city, rather easy-going, freer than Paris. Yet God knows, Evie, how we adored Paris! As if the City made less of a production of itself, in the image of all the Mrs. Shaws on the planet who never try to put themselves on display. A people of limited means who grow tiny flowers in their gardens and form mouths opaque and luminous, so totally human, here below, receivers of the ashes and beauties of this world.

Why then do I not feel comfortable, why have I never felt at ease save in the company of those referred to as people of limited means? Are they my rest, Evie, or my fear? My rest from the furies and the races of this world? Or my fear of confronting the necktie-wearing universe of those who matter?

Did I want so badly to escape the Saint-Henri of my childhood, its unbearable naivety stuffed with overalls and egg sandwiches, to end up in this working-class neighbourhood in North London? Have I escaped all that, tell me, have I escaped the holy pictures and the bleeding Christs of Saint-Henri just so I can live under Mrs. Shaw's crucifix fifty years later? Swapped the kettle on the wood stove for Mrs. Shaw's tea with lemon?

I leave you here, Evie. Now that I'm all mixed up and everything is complicated again.

Craving for jam. For Mrs. Shaw's delicious melon jam.

René

34

FEBRUARY, 1978. New York is coughing slightly in the icy rain, nearly snow, which you might say refuses to be itself, preferring the vague, the in-between, half-water, half-crystal. Accompanied for the past hour by music that's most appropriate for the moment—choral songs and pianoforte, Evelyn too is in a hazy part of existence.

On the phone, Tom O'Leary, who won't let go, never lets go, he's her lover and as obstinate as a grease stain on a pale suit. Evelyn dismisses him awkwardly, not even guiltily, though he's so tender. But his goodness, his doe eyes, his long, languorous lashes make her want to howl, to make insane remarks, to dance on tables. She tells him curtly to stop calling her. Tells him that his gentle voice drives her crazy.

She's sitting on the sofa. Outside, it is raining hazy bodies. Too much body, thinks Evelyn, and not enough being. Above the sofa, a drawing by René: of her, posing naked, on rue Séguier. The pianoforte attacks Saint-Saens.

Exasperated and unable to bear herself, she decides suddenly to call Tom back. She'll come to his place in a while.

"You can come any time, darling."

35

She goes to Tom O'Leary's just like that, taking with her nothing but that formless thing, too nonexistent to be melancholy, that undifferentiated thing that is Evelyn herself. She lacks everything, but nothing in particular. Except perhaps René, but she's not sure. She drives along the New York streets in her Firebird. "Insipid, inconsequential, idle": her three daily conditions. "The same as yesterday and the day before," she thinks. "Unbearable, untenable, insupportable." She chants the words out loud. "Inalienable, untiring, eternal." She smiles. It's been so long since she last smiled. "Watch out! My skin might crack." Her eyes begin to shine.

Suddenly noticing the road sign on her right that reads Interstate 89 North, her fever shoots up—and her speed: now she's turning onto the highway that goes north. "Unjustifiable, inexcusable, unforgivable." Now she is howling with laughter. "Bye-bye, Tom!"

The unending road restores her centre. She has always done this. As if the sequence of white lines could bring order back to her mind. And the endless black pavement, briskly swallowed up, has the ability to soothe her whole being, drawing an unbroken line on her eyes and on her soul at the same time, a line that puts her back together.

As if everything were finally becoming legible.

It's strange, but the road gives her roots, attaches her to the earth, restores her heart. Not the one with ventricles, but the heart that's like the kernel of the enormous fruit whose continents and seas are its pulp.

And when everything was merely chimeras and emptiness, with no more taste or fever, she would still have those astounding trails, at night swept by headlights, to fly away on, the crazy mornings on the main roads at the edge of volcanoes and geysers to carry her away, with harriers flying in the reeds on either side of the super highway.

Born in an age of the horse and carriage, she has never got over that fascination: to move through the countryside at will, to advance as far as she wants on the planet of humans and to do so, in a sense, without moving. Save for her foot stepping onto and off the accelerator. Immobility in movement: the best of both worlds, she thinks.

She is at the wheel of her Firebird as she's at the wheel of her life. A bubble in which, enclosed, she progresses along the roads of the globe, resistant to everything and embracing everything. In a space carefully delimited and on four wheels for confronting the complexity of existence. Bathyscaph with an outline so clean that one can look around inside the riddle of things. Like the image reflected in the rear-view mirror of her Firebird: a short mirror for immeasurable life. Cramped cockpit in the diffracted universe where life can take hold of just one arrival.

Evelyn has always needed the road as a kind of desert island.

Winged island of desert-desires. Place dispensing places, like an offering to the world presented on two columns, on the left and on the right, at two hundred an hour, dust from the long roads that stays on the eyelids. Sense of living which is the sense of being.

She says that there are lovers of love and lovers of the road. And that lovers of love should be jealous, sometimes, of the lovers of the road who are always advancing as if to take a break so as not to lose themselves.

In this rainy night, Evelyn devours Interstate 89 North. Something inside her has grabbed hold of her, her fever coming back with the road.

Now she is flying through the White Mountains. Her wheels throw up behind them two long sprays of droplets, constellations of tears that run away.

The Canadian border is in sight. Or almost.

36

LONDON, 21 FEBRUARY 1978

Mrs. Shaw cried this morning. Softly, without a sound. While talking to me about Deirdre.

At first she refused to see that her little Deirdre's eyes, as tender and round as marbles, were slightly out of whack. Visitors to Brecknock Road could clearly see that those eyes were crossed, crooked, as a result of some curse or other—no one really knew. As for Mrs. Shaw, she simply refused to see and would fly into a muted rage if anyone dared bring up the matter in her presence, even with the greatest tact. The terrible illness was beginning to draw its furrow on Deidre's face. In the form of an incipient strabismus.

Mrs. Shaw cried this morning. Softly, like a Sunday rain.

We were chatting in front of my latest painting. An oil on masonite I'd titled "Mother and Child." Neither the mother nor the child in my picture has eyes.

Mrs. Shaw told me that Deirdre had died upstairs, in her narrow bed with sheets covered with farm animals and studded with stars that she'd embroidered. Above the bed hung a rag doll with serum that had been trickling, drop by drop, for days, into her thin little arm. "She left us like a little chick." Mrs. Shaw didn't add another word.

I couldn't think of anything to say. I've never known how to behave around emotion. The emotion of others is worse. My own, I've usually been able to deal with by playing it down. But other people's, no, that's something I could never do. I'm a kind of illiterate, Evie, where feelings are concerned, do you understand what I'm trying to say? And colours. What colours to give to emotions? I've never known. I have always laid down the colours on my paintings as if I were running away from something. And colours have never been able to catch up with me, attached as I was to sowing them along the way.

But this morning, Evie, I found it. The right colour. I took a fresh brush, the bristles as sleek as a child's hair, and without dipping it into any oil or liquid, I painted eyes for Mrs. Shaw.

In my painting, the mother and child now have eyes. Eyes that only Mrs. Shaw and I can see.

37

HER FRISKY HIGHWAY STEED had brought her to the vicinity of Athelstan. A once prosperous village, entirely Anglophone, not far from Montreal, where certain sworn enemies of the American Revolution, faithful to the British Crown, had taken refuge. Doctor William McLean Rowat had delivered the babies of two generations of women there and throughout his career had ruled as a kind of godfather, learned and wise. Her Grandfather Rowat. Her father's father.

What's left to Evelyn are a few scattered memories of Athelstan, in particular a memory of being bored to death there during her summer holidays, between the obligatory picking of little wild strawberries around the grand-paternal house and the reprimands of her mother—visiting daughter-in-law and currently serving monster-mother, a fearsome wild sow whose complexion in the July sun became dragon's blood, this woman whom no one dared to oppose, not even the patriarch, William Rowat, this woman in whose presence, actually, everyone trembled.

A few specific images, too: the butter factory, a Canadian first, which was the heart of the village activities, and the general store where she would go to dream in front of the endless counter of penny candies. Dream without touching.

Salivate without eating. In Dr. Rowat's house, the penny candies from the general store were inconsistent with a healthy diet. What's more, the daughter-in-law made a point of regularly inspecting the pockets of Evelyn's flowered dresses because now and then, Dr. Rowat himself would drop in three or four pennies intended for sweets.

Her memory keeps intact as well the day, a torrid one, she remembers, when she drew the Athelstan house, sitting among bees and wild rose bushes, under the big Lombardy poplar. In fact, more than her drawing it's the memory of the intoxicating wind in the poplar leaves that she preserves. There are winds that sometimes create you. That curl you against them, laying you down forever in the palm of time, deep in shadows and desires, a magma of horizons still undistinguished and of constantly evolving bedazzlement. There are winds that provoke your birth. Stirrings that beget you, coinciding with those vaster ones that shake up the world; but of those, for the time being, you can only have a premonition.

Evelyn still hears, distinctly, that wind in the leaves of the Athelstan poplars. That strange and enchanting undulation. She sees herself again in the little wall-papered room that leaned against the long tree. Sees herself again isolating with her penumbral eyes the yellow flowers on the wallpaper, then the red flowers, then green and orange, rearranging, realigning, remixing them, her way of waiting for sleep in the rustling roundness where each leaf turns tenderly around itself, swivelling on the axis of its stem that is planted in the bark. Just as the weathervane indicates the wind's direction on the roof of the French Catholic church in the village, the leaves of the Lombardy poplar show Evelyn the way.

Throughout her life, it is the softest sound she'll hear. The trembling of those leaves. Softer even than a day turning pale or lips joining. But of all that, she's not yet aware.

In front of Evelyn's drawing and her excited face, one that her mother has not seen before, a kind of unassailable fortress, her mother offers no comment, even feigns impassivity. But she staggers under the blow. Her dragon's-blood complexion is speckled with small white patches. Sudden vitiligo. Like a sublimated urge.

As for her grandfather, he allows a tear to stand out on his cheek. Evelyn had never seen an adult's tear.

From what then, or for whom perhaps, was her grandfather crying? Evelyn didn't try to find out.

She was, absolutely, in the wind in the poplar.

38

THEY HAVEN'T SEEN EACH OTHER FOR NEARLY SIXTY YEARS. Her first cousin, Heather Rowat Fairbanks, gives her a chilly greeting.

Heather lives in one of those prefab houses that are sprouting across the soil of America, generally in clusters, like little machine-made cakes, adorable little pastry cubes, unaffected by the scorching sun or the pelting rain or the burden of age. Lawns green and smooth as golf courses. Not even one blade sticking out. Freshly disinfected, as if shaven. Protected against all pests, vermin, ragweed, dandelions or blackflies.

The green abundance and the comfortable, rather affluent houses from Evelyn's memory have given way to a kind of misery, humdrum routine wrapped in little acts of meanness squirming like worms, everyday meanness of lands without a future. A kind of poverty covered with melamine.

The general store is still there, but posted outside it now is a plague of motorcycles backfiring amid the vapours from six-packs and barbecue chips. Neither city nor country, neither altogether Montreal nor altogether suburb, no longer really English but not French either, Athelstan lives in a kind of patois-speaking state, neither fish nor fowl, undoing the web of its days and its nights in coils of hotdogs and conjugal violence.

The English have left or are considering it. They are running away from the progress of the Francophones whom history for several years now has allowed to hold their heads up, choosing to decamp in the face of their foretold decline, and their mutation from people of an empire to people of insufficiency.

Now only the old are left. And the mock rockers in their armoured windbreakers, glued to their fake hiccupping Harleys who come to order their beer in Franglais.

Heather's property clashes with the landscape, the only plot that's well-maintained, last square of self-esteem you might say, along with the cemetery where rest the remains of Grandfather Rowat. A cemetery shorn like a poodle. "They don't do it any better at Versailles," Evelyn had laughed to herself.

Heather Rowat Fairbanks has come back to live in Athelstan after her husband's death and twenty years of teaching in Vermont. "I wanted to come home," she explains to her cousin quite simply. She relaxes. What she knows about Evelyn during all those years can be summed up in one sentence: she'd become an artist and she'd married a French Canadian. "And I'm sure you know what the Rowat family thought about artists!" "And about French Canadians!" Evelyn adds. Both women smile. Heather continues, "Artists? They're all drunk and eccentric and lecherous." "And French Canadians?" Evelyn outdoes her. "All elevator boys." At which they share a good laugh. A pregnant pause, surprising them both.

The cousins chat for a while. They talk about their respective occupations. Heather spends her days caring for her plants and baking muffins for her lonely elderly neighbours. But her main fame comes as a bridge player.

"There's just one grocery store in Athelstan, but we have two bridge clubs." Evelyn says that she too adores flowers and plants even though she's not very good with them. She doesn't dare confess that she loathes bridge with every pore of her skin. "I always lose at bridge." Before her cousin, she needs to shrink.

She is reminded of a sentence from the *Journal à quatre mains* by the sisters Benoîte and Flora Groult: "With some people, it is appropriate to lower yourself as if you were getting into a car."

Using as an excuse an appointment in New York that evening, Evelyn soon takes her leave of Heather. Who as a farewell gift places in her cousin's hand two muffins tied with a gold-coloured ribbon. "They're made with oat flour." They were the last words spoken between them. The two women embraced, knowing they would never see one another again.

39

Evelyn escapes from Athelstan, flooring the gas pedal. The way you cut and run from a black bear, noticing nothing around you, staring straight ahead, anticipating—terrified—its teeth ready to bite.

On the passenger seat, Heather's muffins took her breath away. Ridiculous muffins, a metaphor, it seemed to her, for an entire life. That of her cousin and that of Athelstan. Pathetic muffins, offered so cheerfully: which was precisely what made her feel like shedding all the tears in her body.

She was speeding towards New York. The faster she drove, the faster she would burn everything behind her, everything, wipe out all of that insufferable place she's now leaving behind. "You die of boredom and aesthetic poverty first," she told herself. "And from lack of curiosity." She was talking to herself behind the wheel of her Firebird. "Pride of the past, where are you now?" It seemed to her that the dignity of yesteryear, Athelstan's former grace, had drowned in the blue-green waters of a bygone past of which minuscule fringes still persisted in rising to the surface.

She picked up speed, abandoning behind her and using up as she went along the essence of the life that she had wanted to flee since childhood, which she'd glimpsed in all its dazzling intensity in Athelstan—of everything she'd been so passionately determined to escape—first in the arms of the black pianist, Bernard Leshley, then in those of the Saint-Henri painter, René Marcil. Family, isolation, narrow-mindedness, puritanism, conservatism. "Long live the crazy!" she exclaimed aloud, strapped inside her bubble.

She then felt a tremendous surge of love for René. Like the onset of a fever. "What good are our wars, will you tell me?" Briefly, she was stunned by a haze of nostalgia. She gripped the wheel.

At the first rest stop on the highway she braked suddenly, rolled down the window and, filled with guilt to her very bones, tossed the muffins into the garbage can.

Above Interstate 89 South, the sky had darkened again.

On her seat, Evelyn arched her back. She begged the god of the highway to hold her again in his feverish wings.

40

Kilmacrenan, Captain's Bar, 19 December 1979

Melancholy is a form of grace, Evie. I have been thinking about you constantly since I arrived here, in this Ireland where sheep—now blue, now variegated red—graze freely as the birds, standing guard over centuries of peat-burning stoves, of barefoot children, of poets. Where bagpipes and fiddles, chest to chest, are frozen in their powerful sweetness. Where slowness is everywhere, clearer than morning. Where the greys have the power to drive the blue from the sky and from the sea, its unpolished surface, using the blood of wars, each rainfall bringing with it the bitter silt of the rage to live.

Land where opaline days descend into the bars scattered here and there along country back roads, while Guinness and glorious whiskey slip down gullets that are never quenched. It's in one of those seedy dives, polished like a flagship, where the draft beer pump serves as its rudder, that I am writing to you now.

Land of your ancestors on both sides, where melancholy, you told me, is found in mother's milk, along with the mysteries of sky and sea. All I do, Evie, is think about you.

You've often told me that melancholy had formed you, petition to the night, prayer to nothingness, and that this fervour, exercised to no avail, had turned you into a hatmaker, then an artist and designer.

It is here, in this country where the ground beneath our feet rivals nudity itself, it's here that I think I'm beginning to understand what you've so often told me.

Melancholy, Evie, as I understand it, is a ferry that casts off on a Sunday afternoon in autumn when the light is the colour of mustard and our hands twitch continuously, mine and my mother's and my father's, both of them melting into the horizon of the St. Lawrence, which at this level has earned the status of Sea. And it's the truth that my twenty years stay behind on the shore while their fifty years or so move on, and our generations are confounded, tied forever by the thread that unwinds as the ship moves away, feeling a pinch in the heart.

And I go on waving my hand, Evie. Alone on the shore, planted before the vastness of age. And they go on waving theirs. And now, as in a dream, other hands, smaller, younger, have joined mine. Their greetings are addressed to the ship but also, from now on, to me.

Melancholy, Evie, is a ferry that casts off on a Sunday afternoon in autumn.

I send you quite simply my affection, which is profound. Tomorrow I go to Letterkenny to hear old Jeannie Doherty play the fiddle. I take along your ears, your eyes, in the pocket of my overcoat.

René

41

Letterkenny, Central Hotel, 20 December 1979

Take me now, I'm ready. Carry me away, I beg you. Let me dance but do not let me break. And then say nothing more about it. Take away the pieces of me one by one, take them away. But leave my ears here, dear God of Saint-Henri. For the music of old Jeannie, aged ninety-one, her chin fitted into the quavering sound board of the violin, as the Evangeline of the Acadians is forever in the dark nostalgia of the world.

Her wrinkles, slumped onto the instrument, stream to the floor of the Central Hotel, the luminous collapse of a lifetime.

Take away all my pieces, dear God of Saint-Henri, but leave my ears here.

Amen.

Part Five

The Gymnasium on Bloor Street

The Years of Old Age

42

Donegal Town, 21 December 1979

You told me that you'd absorbed melancholy with your mother's milk. That it had been present in the milk of your ancestress, in your great-grandmother's, then your grandmother's, and that it had survived in your mother as well, too concentrated, too intense, melancholy had swept over her as stark, black bile, innervation of harshness and fake frivolity, allocation of armour.

I've never known how to match your melancholy, Evelyn, that meticulous quest for the blood and flesh of the stars. I am nothing but a man who lives. I am the small lantern, flickering in the north wind, who allowed you to keep watch a few times. But I am first and foremost a spoilsport, my own first and then, too often, yours, with my nose to the ground for fear of encountering the sky.

Read me, Evie. Read me while I am still a man who lives.

Love exists only because you read me into existence. Just as the wind exists only because we hear it: I know that now. Love letters are made for the living. Why preserve something we no longer want to read—because they've become pointless, because we can no longer read—because they're too full of the pain of absence?

Hurry and read me, Evie. Read me without flinching. While I am still a man who lives. After that, throw me away.

I go back to London tomorrow. Happy Christmas.

From this small town, the administrative centre of Donegal at the northernmost point of Ireland, which has no charm aside from its claim to being the birthplace of Mrs. Shaw, I am your,

René

43

SHE DANCES SLOWLY, SHE DANCES SO RARELY. In workout clothes moulded tightly to her faded body, she achieves long movements despite her old joints. Bare feet flat on the floor, Evelyn breathes in and out in the middle of the big gymnasium on Toronto's Bloor Street, deserted at this early hour.

Thick makeup, almost too violent for an old woman's transparent skin, is plastered onto her face as protection against the universe. Not for anything would she leave the house without foundation applied in successive coats, a line of kohl traced by a trembling hand around her eyes, and rouge that makes her cheeks as pink as candy. Makeup caked onto her features still filled with night, even though she's been awake for a while now. With age, the facial mask takes longer, so it seems, to cover her daytime furrows.

Evelyn will be eighty-one in a few days' time. With her short white hair, cut flapper-style, and her hunched back, bent at a ninety-degree angle, she has been going to the big Bloor Street gym twice a week. "So they'll bear with me longer," she tells the young doorman at the Sutton Place Hotel who's responsible for getting her a taxi, himself moved, herself hoping to make an impression, and rewarded every time with the same reply: "You're younger than I am, Mrs. Marcil!"

Slowly she sways and undulates and oscillates as though tackling bodily her old back, trying to straighten it even a little and free it from its prison, from its misshapen prostration. After a few seconds' rest, she stretches out her arms in front of her, then spreads them in a long *urbi et orbi* motion, she embraces someone or something or maybe even the earth.

Another pause. There she is again, swaying while she puffs like a heifer about to give birth, this former painter's model, clasped by her withered carcass, as in a Chinese dance in which she is a fine paper dragon.

Contorted in her leotard that reveals all the folds in her flesh, she rocks herself, prostrate on the floor, an old reptile just emerged from who knows where.

The woman who was once the beauty of rue Séguier is beautiful still.

44

Since René's death she's been living on the twenty-fifth floor of Sutton Place, a luxury hotel in downtown Toronto where she has her neighbourhood, her little ways and her court. A court composed basically of elevator attendants, doormen, receptionists and dining room staff. To whom are added a few leeches, imagining they can exploit her fortune, though it now consists of a nest egg barely sufficient to cover her rent and the costs of storing, maintaining and promoting the thousands of paintings that make up the body of work of René Marcil.

Her apartment—from which one can look down at the cars tumbling along the streets like green peas in a serving dish—is a dense forest whose trees and branches and leaves are so many of René's paintings, carefully arranged, laid out in graduated ranks from smallest to largest. Not to mention those that cover the walls. They fill every centimetre of her home.

At night she falls asleep under the "Pont de chemin de fer" that her husband painted in 1953, in Vence. The bridge spans rain forests where she dreams, while at the same time, sleeping beneath the bedposts along with her are canvases from the period of the south of France. "René's mauve period," she likes to say.

Sleeping at her side as well are a brand-new computer, her clothes for the Bloor Street gym and a tiny cedar box that holds letters nearly a hundred years old. All dated 1905. Written in San Francisco by her maternal grandfather, Joseph. Her sister had given them to her on Naomi's death because she "didn't know what to do with them."

Except for those things, the rest of the universe could go up in smoke.

Muffled in her tower that she leaves only for business reasons—René's business—Evelyn lives the life of a rude old woman, always ready to become indignant or to fly off the handle in her own particular way.

She's the one who every day—while the diners at other tables look on, appalled—takes away her leftovers in a doggy bag: cold, shrivelled fried potatoes, small amounts of salad and tomatoes, three or four mouthfuls of beef or chicken, bread, butter and condiments. With a knowing wink from Consuelo: "This is my lunch for tomorrow." She's also the one who can be heard liberally chewing out the doorman—"her" doorman—if the taxi is so unfortunate as to pull up a little late to drive her to the Bloor Street gym.

And again, it is she who one day is seen urging an attendant to centre the bouquet that adorns a Louis XVI sideboard in the lobby. She comes back to life when the employee shifts the flowers a few centimetres. "Phew!" It's the whole hotel that starts to breathe again.

45

Deep in her sanctuary of oils and charcoal, Evelyn is hunched over a blue screen. *Enter*. Her owl eyes, slightly glassy, hunt intently for the cursor. *Enter*. She talks to herself, "Oooh! Come on, honey!" *Enter*. Her old chest wheezes, makes a series of odd little sounds like those of a suckling baby. *Enter*. Finally there appears on the screen the menu she wants. Jubilation. "Thank God." *Enter*.

She spends her days indexing every one of René's paintings: title, where created, date. As meticulous as an archivist. It's Consuelo, a waiter in the dining room, but more important, a young painter in need of money, who talked her into buying a computer. She, Evelyn, age eighty-one, woman of another century, venturing into cyberspace.

She doesn't want to die before the painter René Marcil has gained recognition for what he is: "A very great painter," she repeats to Consuelo incessantly, in a tone that brooks no rejoinder, displaying to him for the umpteenth time the old letter from the Guggenheim Museum: "I was struck by the large still life which you very kindly left at the Museum." True to her habits, she has ordered a coffee—"Very hot, please!"—which she'll gulp, generally ice-cold, with a multitude of vitamin pills. "A giant of painting, Consuelo!" The young man, anticipating the slightest wish of the duchess of the twenty-fifth floor, will smile.

Evelyn is busy with the paintings: identifying, filing, if necessary mounting and framing them. Sometimes she'll even travel to see anyone she thinks is seriously interested in the painter: critics, gallery owners, curators, collectors.

She doesn't want to vanish from this earth without doing all she can to make known and appreciated the work of the painter René Marcil.

46

René had spent the last two years of his life under Evelyn's roof, in Toronto. True to form: pencil and paper at his fingertips. His sketches had become light, some were even humorous, as if he were letting himself go—or quite simply letting go.

Evelyn had felt charged with the responsibility of ensuring René's artistic legacy, his life after death. She had accepted the torch of that posterity quite naturally, just as she'd guaranteed René's material support for fifty years. Seeing to his interests after death as she'd done during his lifetime seemed to her self-evident.

René Marcil died on September 25, 1993, at Mount Sinai Hospital in Toronto, accompanied by the utter indifference of the artistic community, the press and all the rest of thinking humanity.

One of his last drawings was made for Evelyn at his bedside, four long letters on a large white sheet of paper: E-V-I-E, and at the bottom, in tiny letters: l-o-v-e. Never before, for her or for anyone else, had he put together those four diminutive letters.

47

On the day of his cremation, Evelyn learned that Mount Sinai had received as a donation a large piece by René Marcil, which would be placed prominently in the vast lobby on University Street.

Nicolas, a friend of Evelyn's, had gone to deliver the canvas and to pick up René's things. In no particular order he took shaving foam, sketchbooks, pyjamas, dressing gown and two photos: one of Mrs. Shaw in front of her house on Brecknock Road, the other, yellowed and tattered, taken in 1966 at Cabrières d'Aigues, of himself sketched by Evelyn while he was painting on the ground, crouched in the grass and thyme, both knees on his canvas to keep it safe from the wind.

Part Six

Gracia

48

SAN FRANCISCO, 1 MAY 1905

Dearest Naomi,

I've gone. You are seven years old. I'm twenty-seven. My friend Gracia is sixty-seven.

Your father has run away, Naomi. To California. With Gracia. To a better elsewhere, one that's more risky maybe, but then I'm more clear-sighted, too, knowing that for you nourishment—that of the body in any event, which will make you grow in grace and beauty—is guaranteed. Your mother is a good mother.

Don't turn the bitterness, the anger you may feel towards me, against yourself, Naomi, please try not to do that.

I write to you now though I know that you won't read this. Not in the short term in any case. Because you'll be prevented, and you'll be kept in the most impenetrable ignorance of what has motivated me. Yet my words exist because I can hear them tracing their grooves on the paper. They'll come to you along a path that's impossible for me to imagine just yet. But one way or another, they will reach you.

I want you to be as free as the egret that flies across the hoop of the sun. I want you to feel the same freedom. Will you be up to it, Naomi? Or will your time, the time that's allotted to you, run out as you search for that freedom, so that the time of those who will come after can imbue it with the complex perfumes of their eyes?

You'll probably never read these lines, my darling child. But the work of freedom, which is so close to that of happiness, may perhaps spill onto the roads you'll take and roll you in their pebbles. It's from the darkest night, you know, that the brightest stars emerge. It is from the blind wind that sends their seeds tumbling into the blue sky that flowers grow.

One day, Naomi, I saw a hat fly away in the wind, then land on the head of someone quietly making her way through the crowd, her steady footsteps following the path laid out by the throng. The life of that passer-by, I'm sure of it, was changed by that event forever.

We can invent our lives, Naomi. Despite the balls and chains we drag along, that age accumulates, I think, until someone drains them of their substances, a massive cleaning. You'll have to invent your own with the ball-and-chain that I will always represent for you until the end of your life and maybe even beyond. I'll be the cross you have to bear, Naomi, you will try to find me everywhere, you'll wander from ersatz to substitute in search of the colour of your soul, and it will be hard for you to love on account of a father who went away to save himself when you were seven years old.

But we do go away, Naomi. We can reach the point of going away to redeem ourselves.

Now, don't suppose that it's Gracia, whose love is more important to me than myself, who has saved me. Love does not bring salvation. It is the power of love that saves us. Which is in fact the power of being oneself.

I kiss your hair, my little carrot-top. And I lull you to sleep with my Ireland.

Joseph, your father,
who will cherish you forever
who will miss you like
a ventricle of his heart.

49

To Gracia, San Francisco, 27 July 1905

I Found You

I found you aging and tender,
your boar's heart gnawed by wolves,
ripe as a melon's ripe
and in wait for me

I found you gorged with juices,
your noble rot scaled my heart,
tan lacquered grapes
upon a trellis

I loved you when it was not too late,
your skin so fine it threatened to split
and engulf me in its flesh,

heart silk gone tender with the years,
mellow from each time before me
that someone, bird, man, woman, child,
nestled at your hip, drank your lips,
nested in your folds

I found wrinkles about your eyes,
skin flecked with the blood of days,
unburdened by excess,
set free from the sublime,
I found you undone by all,
endlessly reshaped, shaped with your naked hands,
cippus of opal on the dark earth,
wandering come home from away

I saw you before you saw me,
moon risen through the spruce
with the sun not yet set

I gathered you before you culled me,
soft rose gone wild,
I had but to take you,
unfurl myself on your mouth

I fished you at the still tide,
slow fold under waves of sand,
fold held there by the sea,
unhurried

I loved you already formed, made elsewhere,
strongly made,
fine dough between my fingers of clay

I found you a poem, alive
in the sun, reading me pages fanned by time,
under your woolens with your wide-rimmed eyes
taking sorrow in vain.

I found you before the herons pass,
before the buzzard brushes our feet with mist,

before the grasses snap
and the willow-herbs fly like snow

I found you one russet morning
in the bed where moose
force their brood outside,
trump rosy farewells in song

I found your warm lion's womb,
begetter of milk-pale deserts,
bolt ajar
on the long scar
of ancient quarterings

I found you alive, brought down
before you found me
and never more will I find such a one[6]

Joseph

50

To Gracia, San Francisco, 27 September 1905

HAPPINESS

Happiness does not know where to lay down its wild head, on the prominent shoulders of the not-so-distant Sierra Nevada, or the long neck of the San Joaquin River, or the warm hip of San Francisco Bay that's open onto Pacific dreams. My heart runs from rock flowers to freshwater flowers to sea flowers, not knowing where to fall again because of its old weariness and its new adulation.

Where to lay it down, Gracia, tell me, between the frightening sweetness of love, a drop of pale whisky and another of Liszt, like a fresh wound?

Where to lay down the flowers of happiness—in what vase, what meadows, what grove of elms so they won't fade or dry out, so they'll take off to decorate the earth with the wind?

Where to lay down the waters of happiness, overflow of springs and springtime, so they won't dry up, won't run dry, but will instead nourish char and trout?

Where to lay down the words of happiness, in what ink, on what velvety vellum? Where to lay them down, Gracia, tell me, if not in a few bosoms of childhood, dwarf knolls initiated into the mystery of beauty by grandmotherly peaks?

That no doubt is why humans refuse to depart this life. Because of those forms of happiness. Because of those delights. Plenty of humus and asphalt for sidewalks. Plenty of flies, crickets, car horns. Plenty of lines to hang up in the evening wind. And seedy bars with warm breath where smoky humanity quenches its thirst for itself.

That may also be why certain humans, in love with love and with permanence, aspire to reproduce, to create some light to perpetuate the chain of fervour and exultation. To pour the ambrosia of the sublime onto some fresh, intact face, greedy for the poetry of life.

Powerful bits of food: transmitting the knowledge of love, a short golden thread in the fabric of time.[7]

Until then I couldn't imagine what it is that drives men and women to want to reproduce, to re-produce, by themselves, in small wailing flasks that are good to fill. With what? I had no idea.

Yet I do have offspring, Gracia, my little Naomi, a lock of whose red hair I've shown you so many times and which I keep with me always, a little Naomi born when I did not yet know the light.

It is because of such happiness no doubt that the living miss their dead so much. Sharing of delights smashed to bits forever, communion slashed like slits in the mountains.

And it's why paradise itself misses the stretch marks of earth.

It's time now for phosphorescent wildlife,
We are already in the shadows, Gracia,
But the San Joaquin is a survivor of the light.

Joseph

Part Seven

The Hat

51

Toronto. Late afternoon in autumn. An old woman walks along Wellesley Street. It's windy. She strides decisively, a large drawing case under her arm, her hand struggling to keep a broad-brimmed hat on her head.

Her bent back that stoops her shoulders is parallel to the sidewalk. It seems bowed under by the weight of several lifetimes.

Leaves fallen from the trees swirl on the street. As if they've been sucked up to the sky and no longer tolerate the earth. The gust of wind on the old woman encounters no obstacle but her hat.

Behind a long building made of crushed glass, the big drawing case soon disappears from sight just as the old woman turns the corner at Bay Street, stepping into the night.

Epilogue

FEBRUARY IN THE YEAR 2001. Are you dead, Evelyn, or still alive? I stand on the flank of the Luberon, those mountains like she-bears who've dropped dead at the mauve hour. The deep purple night goes down to the Mediterranean, bypassing like the water your beloved Mont Sainte-Victoire.

Your soul is gliding, so close, so close to me, your soul is fluttering above this country, France, to which you wanted so much to return. You will come back, Evelyn, not alive, but dead, in my hands that tomorrow will lay you down, in a dream, in Père Lachaise, where you dreamed of resting, you were so close to it, Evelyn.

The sun is setting. And the moon is rising. I am exactly equidistant from the two, if I hold my arms out I can touch the two poles of your life. And set you down there, in the very middle.

Your soul is mauve and it has a daughter, Evelyn. The one you yourself nearly had. Very close to here. Your little Marie would be fifty years old now. You wanted a daughter because of melancholy, you'd told me. The melancholy of women bent forever over cradles and graves. Over daisies that have tumbled from their aprons and the big and little wounds to be dressed.

And your daughter, Evelyn, why would she write?

To give back a little of the light that's come from far beyond her. To pay tribute to the mauve hour.

Notes

1. This translation of Antoine Gérin-Lajoie's "Un Canadien errant" is by Edith Fowke:

> Once a Canadian lad,
> Exiled from hearth and home,
> Wandered, alone and sad,
> Through alien lands unknown.
> Down by a rushing stream,
> Thoughtful and sad one day,
> He watched the water pass
> And to it he did say:
>
> "If you should reach my land,
> My most unhappy land,
> Please speak to all my friends
> So they will understand.
> Tell them how much I wish
> That I could be once more
> In my beloved land
> That I will see no more.
>
> "My own beloved land
> I'll not forget till death,
> And I will speak of her
> With my last dying breath.
> My own beloved land
> I'll not forget till death,
> And I will speak of her
> With my last dying breath."

2. Gabrielle Roy.

3. Jean Giono.

4. Stig Dagerman.

5. Henry James.

6. The translation of Joseph's poem to Gracia is by Donald Winkler.

7. Penelope Lively.

Acknowledgements

The Canada Council for the Arts
Centre national du livre de France
Jean-Jacques Boin
Yves Bisaillon
Michel Morin
Famille Audigier
Edmée de Villebonne
Sabine Tamisier
Alain Letaille